An Ice Way to Die

A Julia Greene Travel Mystery

by

Linda Clayton

For information, email **Cozy Cat Press**, cozycatpress@aol.com or visit our website at: www.cozycatpress.com

COZY CAT
P R E S S

ISBN: 978-1-946063-02-1

Printed in the United States of America

Cover design by Paula Ellenberger
www.paulaellenberger.com

1 2 3 4 5 6 7 8 9 10

Dedication:

For all eleven of you. You know who you are.

LARK TOURS:
YOUR PASSPORT TO ADVENTURE
AND EXCITEMENT

Lark Tours welcomes you to an exciting glimpse of mystical, beautiful Iceland. Sit back in the comfortable seat of our luxury bus, enjoy the scenery and learn a bit about the folklore and customs of our land. Did you know there are hidden people, or huldufólk, and trolls living in the trees and rocks? Perhaps you will see one. We have also provided a list of your fellow passengers to help you get acquainted. We hope you have a wonderful trip full of lasting memories.

Passenger List

1. *Renee and Arnold (Skip) Alessio*   *Akron, OH*
2. *Serge and Nicole Boucher*   *Walnut Creek, CA*
3. *Lydia and Cameron Cumberland San Francisco, CA*
4. *Olivia Duncan*   *Wake Forest, NC*
5. *Angela Fratello*   *Tulsa, OK*
6. *Julia Greene*   *Wake Forest, NC*
7. *Dirk Harrison*   *Sacramento, CA*
8. *Ginger and George Reilly*   *Pittsburgh, PA*
9. *Emma and Nathan Sperling*   *Muncie, IN*

Christof Gunarsson will be your knowledgeable guide. We hope you don't encounter any problems, but if you should, Christof will know what to do.

CHAPTER 1

A sudden wind howled across the top of the volcano, and within seconds we were engulfed in a blinding ash whiteout.

"You all please stop walking," our guide yelled. "Do not try to get back to the bus. Do you hear me? Do not walk. It is too dangerous."

A hint of panic tinged Christof's voice. He didn't need to worry. I wasn't about to go stumbling around the slippery surface of the Solheimjökull glacier. I dug the crampons attached to my shoes into the ice, intending to stay put.

Olivia Duncan, my best friend, grabbed my arm. Her hat had blown off her head and her tangled chestnut hair was already covered in ash. She leaned close and yelled into my ear, "This is not my idea of fun. Let's make a run for it."

"And go where?" I shouted. We had driven at least two miles over organ-jolting volcanic rock and dirt to reach the glacier. And we had hiked at least twenty-five minutes on its surface. Also, Olivia and I weren't exactly built for speed, so running over mounds of ice might be a problem. Olivia was gorgeous—flawless skin that tanned easily, huge dark eyes, and the aforementioned luxurious chestnut hair, but her days of frolicking gaily across the meadow wearing a skimpy sundress were over. So were mine. My body showed vestiges of my former athletic days, but I couldn't touch my toes if a thousand-dollar bill waved at me from the ground right in front of me. So running was out.

"We should stay with the group. This probably won't last long," I told her.

But what did I know? I, Julia Greene, was not an expert on volcanic activities. As a matter of fact, I wasn't much of an expert on anything—except food, and I only say this because I love to eat it and cook it. I will put my chocolate fudge dream cake with caramel swirl icing up against all comers.

Olivia and I owned Little Bites, a lunch and sweet shop in Wake Forest, North Carolina. We served sandwiches, two kinds of quiches and a variety of excellent baked goods. Our customers were particularly fond of my profiteroles, which were filled with a scrumptious custard cream and drizzled with hot fudge sauce. And the only eruption we ever had to deal with was when the top of the blender exploded. Scraping mango filling off the ceiling was not an easy or pleasant task.

Now the wind was blowing so hard, I kept my head down and wrapped my arms around my body. This felt exactly like a snow whiteout I'd experienced as a child back in Cleveland. Except instead of fluffy clean snow, it was ash—dirty black ash—that was now in my eyes and mouth and coated my jacket.

It took forever for the wind to die down. When it did, I cautiously opened my eyes and looked around. The others were doing the same. We all were covered in so much ash, we resembled some kind of extraterrestrial beings.

Christof scurried among us. "Is everyone okay? Quite an experience, was it not? The ash was sitting on top of the volcano up there"—he gestured to the famous Eyjafjallajökull—"just waiting for a little breeze to come by and blow it off. Just a little something to add to your adventure in Iceland."

There were fourteen of us on this amazing trip. Even though we had only known each other for a few days, I had already formed some opinions. Take Emma and Nathan Sperling, for instance. Emma was probably a lovely woman, but I knew she and I would not be exchanging email addresses when the trip was over. She was a bit bossy, annoyingly nosy and incessantly chatty. Short, square and solidly built, she had frizzy brown hair and a round face. Her husband, a thin angular man, carried his wife's tote bag, which contained colored pencils, bits of sewing, little note books and small, mysterious opaque bottles. He was a strong defender of his wife but otherwise never said much, probably because his wife wouldn't let him.

As usual, she began talking before Christof could finish. "I'd like to take some of this ash back to the States. This will make such an interesting topic at my Friday morning Stitch and Chat group. Would you all mind waiting while I collect some?"

"No! Some of us want to get out of here." Skip Alessio took off his Cleveland Indians cap and banged it against his leg. Skip was probably 6'3," tan and muscular. He had blond hair, a hearty laugh and really white teeth. I suspected muscle mass had replaced some of his brain cells. He called his wife "kiddo" and showed off his strength by trying to hoist some of the ladies into the air. His unsuccessful attempt with Olivia had resulted in a bloody nose—his.

"Don't know why you always have to hold up the trip. It would be great if we could get through a day without having to stop to stare at a bird or a cloud or some pile of rocks."

His wife, Renee, nodded in agreement. "This wind is awful for my hair. And I don't want to see another bird—unless it's one of those cute little puffers."

"It's a puffin, not a puffer, and they are all gone this time of year." Nathan Sperling put his arm around his wife's shoulder. "And you'd know that if you'd read the print-out my wife prepared for you."

Renee ignored him. She pulled the hood of her jacket off her head and shook out her hair. "Ugh! I've got ash everywhere. Skip, be a sweetie and brush it off me."

Her husband did as he was asked, and the group watched in fascination as clouds of black ash flew off her long blond locks. Renee was probably a perky size zero and had a compact, toned body, which she could never resist showing off. She liked to share that her "smoking hot self" was the result of her job as a fitness instructor. She told us she was a "Georgia peach," and when she remembered, she left the *g* off the ends of her words.

Ginger and George Reilly, or *The Twins*, as Olivia and I called them, stood with Nicole and Serge Boucher. The Reillys both had red hair, fair skin and blue eyes and looked enough alike to be brother and sister. But they were listed on the passenger manifest as *Mr.* and *Mrs.* and they spent a lot of time canoodeling, so it appeared to be some fluke of chromosomal coincidence that made then resemble each other so strongly. At least I hoped so.

I had no idea about Nicole and Serge Boucher. I guessed they were both in their early sixties. Aside from sharing they were from California, they volunteered nothing more about themselves. Both dressed completely in black—black turtle neck sweaters and pants and huge black sunglasses that obscured most of their faces.

"Listen, people," Angela Fratello's voice boomed over our chatter. "You're scaring the *huldufólk*. If you quiet down, we might be able to see them. They live here, you know. You're not being respectful."

"She's nuts," Olivia muttered. "Look at her. Who dresses like that to walk on a glacier?"

Angela stood on the ice with her arms raised above her head. The flaps on the thick wool cap she was wearing flared at the sides like bat wings. The hem of her long skirt was soaking wet and caked with dirt. I sighed. From the first meeting at JFK, Angela had done her best to annoy everyone. She was loud and opinionated and very hard to talk to.

"Will you stop with the *huldufólk* crap," George yelled. "I'm sick and tired of listening to you talk about hidden people. Maybe you should go see if you can find them."

Our tour leader looked distressed. "Now, now. Let us try to be nice. The hidden people are interesting to talk about, but maybe not now." He looked hopefully at Angela. "We should slowly start walking to the bus."

"Oh, the secrets this glacier must hold," Angela's stentorious voice boomed, "in the shadows of the Eyjafjallajökull, which has been awakened by the spirits."

"Put a sock in it," someone yelled.

"Yeah, Angela, get moving."

"Where's Lydia? Has anyone seen my wife?" Cameron Cumberland stumbled toward us, a panicked look on his face. "Have you seen her? I can't find her."

Answers of "nope" and "sure haven't" only made Cameron more upset. He turned the color of chalk and began to shake visibly.

We crowded around him asking questions until Christof took control. "When did you notice she was not with you? Please do not worry. She is surely somewhere behind us."

"She isn't. When the ash began blowing, I put my head down and tried to walk forward. She was holding onto the back of my jacket." Pure fear flooded his voice. "I don't know when she let go. I was concentrating so hard on moving forward... My God, where can she be?"

I turned and looked behind me. The cold glacier resembled a desolate moonscape of ice, lava rock and black ash from the recent eruption. It looked rugged and sinister and walking on it, even with crampons, was not one of my favorite things to do. I remembered Lydia was wearing a red jacket, a purple knit hat and a green scarf around her neck. As I scanned the glacier, there was no speck of color moving over the ice.

Christof's face was grim as he hitched his backpack higher and adjusted his sunglasses. "You all wait here. I will find her and be right back."

Cameron fell into step beside him. "You're not going without me."

"Me, either," Skip announced. "Six eyes are better than four."

"You're not leaving me here." Renee slid her hand into her husband's. "I'm coming, too."

"We'll all go," Dirk Harrison said. "It's better to stay together. We don't want to lose someone else." He smiled, but there was concern in his eyes. There was something about him that made others listen to what he said—as if he was used to giving commands. He, too, hadn't offered much personal information. He was a lawyer from Sacramento, California, and that was all we knew.

"My feet hurt," Ginger complained. "I wish I could take off these crampons."

"Well, don't," her husband advised. "I don't want you to slip and fall."

As usual, the Bouchers said nothing. Since both wore oversized sunglasses, it was impossible to read their expressions.

Olivia and I hung back as others filed past us. "What are we waiting for?" my friend asked. "Are we going to run for the bus?"

"No, that's not a good idea. Were you with me when the wind began to blow? I remember shutting my eyes and feeling a bit disoriented."

My friend considered this. "I think I was."

"Did you see the Cumberlands?"

"I don't think so. They were behind me. Honestly, Julia, I wasn't paying much attention to anything. I was trying to keep my head down and not ingest ash."

"And I was trying to avoid Angela," I told her. "I actually ran away from her at one point."

Olivia nodded. "I can certainly understand that. There's one on every tour, isn't there? One person who doesn't seem to be able to fit in with the group. I'll bet she lives a lonely life without many friends."

Emma Sperling bustled up to us and said, "I wish I were with Lydia. She must be terrified right now." Her mouth pursed into a disapproving line. 'Although I must say, her husband should have taken better care of her. Nathan would never abandon me."

"I'll bet he'd like to, though," Olivia said under her breath.

Emma's pink cheeks turned bright red. "I was only trying to help. That's a very unkind thing to say, Olivia." She appealed to Ginger, who was zipping her jacket. "Some people are so cruel."

"Oh, for heavens sake! I'm not being cruel," Olivia said. "Your comments just aren't helpful at the moment. I didn't mean to hurt your feelings."

Mollified, Emma scuttled away. "So," I continued, "it seems Lydia was the last one on the path. Surely if she had tripped or fallen she would have called out for her husband."

"But he may not have heard her," Olivia countered. "The wind was so strong and we all had hoods or hats pulled over our ears."

"Nevertheless, something has happened to her," I whispered to my friend, "otherwise, why isn't she with us?"

We stopped talking and fell into step with the others. Heavy gray clouds hung over the top of the Eyjafjallajökull, the volcano responsible for disrupting so much air traffic in 2010. Black ash covered sharp edges of ice, and chunks of lava rock made walking difficult. When the sun disappeared, it was suddenly cold. To make matters worse, an icy spray of rain stung our faces. This definitely was not fun. Iceland was an intriguing and awesome country, but I longed for a shower and clothes that weren't covered in ash.

We all stopped when Renee yelled, "Look! There's a green scarf. See it down there?" She pointed to a crevice twenty feet below where we stood. "Wasn't Lydia wearing a green scarf? I'm sure she was because I remember wondering where she bought it. I mean it looked kind of cheap but I figured it must have been expensive because she has that Louboutin handbag."

We watched as Christof ran down the slope. Less agile, Cameron tried to follow him and fell hard onto his knees. George sidestepped down the hill to him and pulled him to his feet.

"Let me go," Cameron demanded. "I have to get down there." As he tried to get away from George, he lost his footing again, and they both went down.

Renee ran down the glacier like a Swiss mountain goat. "Get out of my way, you idiots. Go back up to the path where you can't get hurt," she yelled as she passed the men.

"You go if you want to," I said to Olivia. "I get vertigo just looking down. And I value my limbs far too much to attempt the descent."

Angela loomed behind us. "Ah, she's probably down there talking to one of the trolls. There are two living in the ice, you know." She smiled, exhibiting teeth that resembled those of a recent Kentucky Derby participant. I tired to ignore her, but that was difficult. She poked me in the side with her walking stick. "Maybe you could get your special friend to lend you a hand."

I sighed. Ever since Dirk Harrison invited me—and four others, I might add—to have cocktails before dinner our first night in Reykjavik, Angela had been suggesting Dirk Harrison was my "special friend."

Actually, I didn't think I wanted a "special friend." Ever since my husband had died two years ago, I'd been finding my way as a suddenly single woman, and I didn't need a man muddying up the process. To be honest, there were still times when I woke up in the middle of the night crying and thinking about him, which probably meant I wasn't yet ready for any kind of romantic entanglement. But, life goes on, and I certainly intended to do the same. And in spite of all my protestation, I had to admit there was a certain spark between Dirk and me. I felt it as soon as we met. It was an instant attraction that was difficult to explain, but nevertheless there.

Angela pulled a tattered copy of *Icelandic Folk and Fairy Tales* from her jacket pocket. Her intention was clear. She was going to educate us.

Vertigo be damned! "Got to go, Angela. No time to chat."

I took a deep breath and started down the slope of the glacier, astounded that I preferred broken bones to a lecture from Angela. I reached the others in time to see

Christof bend over something. When Cameron let out an almost primal scream, I knew they had found Lydia.

CHAPTER TWO

She was lying on her back on the ice, her head twisted in an impossible position. Cameron bent over her, slapping her face over and over, imploring, "Come on, honey. Come on. You're just cold. Stand up!"

But she wasn't cold. She was dead. I knew this because her blue eyes were open and unblinking and stared at nothing. Next to me, Renee shivered uncontrollably and wrapped her arms around her body in an attempt to stop the shaking.

"Her lips are blue. That's horrible. I mean, that can't be from the cold because strictly speaking, she can't be cold, can she? And she isn't wearing her crampons. That was dumb. I'll bet she slipped and fell."

One by one, everyone but Angela managed to come down the hill. Shocked at the sight of Lydia lying on the ground, we huddled in little groups, stunned at finding one of our group suddenly gone.

"I suggest we try to call for help," Dirk Cameron said to Christof. "Do you have a way to contact a hospital or the police?"

Our guide pulled out a walkie-talkie. "I can call the bus driver. He can alert the authorities."

Serge Boucher bent down and put his fingers on Lydia's neck. He looked at Dirk and shook his head. Rising slowly to his feet, he said, "Her body under those clothes is still warm, meaning she hasn't been gone for very long."

Cameron flew at Serge and tried to hammer him with his fists. "Don't touch my wife. And don't talk like that. If you touch her again, I'll kill you."

"Relax, man." Skip put his beefy arm around the distraught man's shoulder and pulled him away. "That dude is a doctor. He isn't doing anything wrong. Think about it. If he were up to something, would he pick this butt hole of the earth place to do it?"

Olivia shook her head. "My, you certainly have a way with words." To the assembled group, she said, "Who has something alcoholic to drink?" When no one replied, she said, "Come on, folks. Not one of you has some kind of liquid libation with you? This poor guy could really use a drink. Look at him."

Cameron's face was the color of paste. He was so distraught Skip had to physically restrain him from lying down on the ice next to Lydia.

"I have some brandy. It's purely for emergency, like sterilizing a wound and such. I, myself, would certainly never touch it." Emma pulled a silver flask out of her backpack and handed it to Skip, who coaxed Cameron to take a swallow.

"Mighty fancy container for an emergency supply," Olivia whispered, "but you can't look a gift horse in the mouth." Aloud she said, "Thank you, Emma. I'm sure that will help him."

Christof contacted the bus driver, who said there was no cell phone reception where the bus waited, and it would take at least an hour for him to find help and another hour to get back to us. It would be dark by the time he returned. We debated what to do.

"I, for one, can't stay here any longer," Renee said. "I'm freezing. Why can't we go back to the bus?" She gestured at Lydia. "We can't do anything for her. Why can't we leave her here?" She looked at our shocked faces and said, "What's wrong with you all? Get real, people. She's beyond anybody's help."

She had a point—not about leaving Lydia here, because that was unthinkable. But we couldn't stay here much longer. It was cold, and the rain was coming down harder. I needed to talk to Dirk alone so I waited until he finished talking to Christof, then pulled him aside and said, "Maybe we could bring Lydia up and take her back to the bus. It sounds gruesome, but we need to get out of this weather, and she can't stay behind. You and Muscle Man and Christof are strong enough to carry her. I don't know about the good doctor and George and Nathan Sperling. Cameron will probably insist on helping, but I don't think he should."

He nodded. "I agree. The driver said there are warm blankets on the bus. We just have to figure out how to do this."

"Why don't I try to round up the ladies and head to the bus? Maybe the driver could start walking to meet us, in case I'm not sure of the way."

He looked at me uncertainly. "Do you think you know how to get back?"

"How hard can it be? We'll do fine. I'm counting heavily on one of us having a good sense of direction."

Dirk laughed, but I wasn't joking. I was happy to hear the other women were agreeable to my plan. They weren't crazy about riding back with a recently deceased Lydia, but they were also beginning to freeze. As soon as we saw the men prepare to lift Lydia off the ice, we started walking. Olivia said she had the homing instincts of a carrier pigeon, so she led the way. The others fell in behind her and I brought up the rear. We had only gone a few feet when I realized Angela wasn't with us.

"Hold up," I called. "We're missing someone."

As if she heard me, a voice boomed from somewhere to the right. Two hundred yards away, Angela stood on the top of a huge, jagged rock. How she managed to get up there in her long skirt and assorted accessories was something probably only the hidden people knew. She threw her arms up to the sky and bellowed, "Hear us, oh, trolls and *huldufólk*. Share with us your secrets. We are ready to receive."

Olivia stomped to the edge of the precipice, put her hands on her hips and yelled, "Righto, Angela. We're leaving now. You stay there if you want to, but we're not coming back for you. Up to you."

Angela appeared to ignore us, and for a few minutes I was afraid we were going to have to haul her off the rock. Without looking back, we began to walk, and out of the corner of my eye, I saw her turn around and cautiously climb down. She stayed a distance behind us, which was fine with me. I was definitely not in the mood for conversation.

Later, when we'd all arrived at the bus, I waited as Renee, Ginger and Nicole mounted the steps of the bus ahead of me. As Ginger attempted to crawl into the seat next to her husband, her tote bag fell out of her hand and clattered to the ground. Emma sprang to her feet to help, knocking her Vera Bradley bag off her lap. As she bent down to pick up her things, she accidentally banged into Renee, who was standing in the aisle. The contents of her canvas tote added to the pile on the floor.

I looked down in dismay at the jumble of spilled belongings. Ginger dove into the pile, picking up a lipstick and assorted packages of candy. I tried to help by picking up objects that had rolled under seats.

"Give that to me," Emma demanded. I held a blue smurf in my hand. "It's my good luck charm. I never travel without it."

"That's fine, Emma," I said, handing it back to her. "We could all use some good luck on this trip."

By silent consent we all sat in the front of the bus and tried to avoid looking at the last row of seats where Lydia lay. She was covered with a blanket, but the unmoving shape was almost worse than seeing her on the ice. Cameron sat next to her, and no amount of talking could persuade him to leave her side. Emma scurried back and forth, bringing him water, a wet cloth for the headache she presumed he had, and a shawl from her hand luggage. She scowled at anyone who attempted to speak to the bereaved man.

Dirk slid into the seat across the aisle from me and said, "I talked to Christof. We're taking her to a clinic in Vik. The driver thinks we can get there faster than an ambulance could meet us. The police will want some information, too."

"I feel so sorry for Cameron," I said. "How in the world could this happen? If she had been holding onto her husband's shirt, what made her let go? She must have screamed when she fell. Why didn't we hear it?"

"Good questions." He pulled two energy bars out of his backpack and offered me one. When I shook my head, he said, "Better eat it. I have a feeling dinner is going to be very late tonight."

I looked at the others seated around me. "No one saw or heard anything. That just doesn't seem possible. I wasn't anywhere near Cameron and Lydia, but The Twins were. So were Nicole and Serge Boucher." I took a bite of the energy bar and thought about the Cumberlands. They were the only two who hadn't flown with us from JFK and so had missed getting acquainted with the group at the airport. Once the tour started, they kept pretty much to themselves.

"It was blowing hard," I said. "And we were all concerned with keeping our heads down and staying upright. The wind could have ripped her screams away."

I shuddered. That was a terrible image—a woman falling and calling out for help, knowing her plea was being swallowed in the wind. I closed my eyes and tried to erase the image of Lydia lying lifeless on the glacier. No luck, though. It was permanently burned into my retinas. I opened my eyes when Ginger sat down in the seat in front of me and buried her face in her hands. Even though I didn't know her well, I liked her, and I recognized someone in need of comforting. I got up and plopped down next to her.

"If I'm intruding you can tell me to go away, but you look like you could use a hug."

She swiped at her tears with a paper towel. "Sorry. George isn't very good at sympathizing with people. I suppose he means well, but..."

"Men get embarrassed when they have to share emotions. This is an awful situation. We should all be crying."

She still looked miserable. "It's just that she"—she jerked her head toward the back of the bus—"and I had an argument yesterday. It was over such a silly thing. George told a joke and Lydia said it was offensive." She looked down at her hands. "I don't know. Maybe it was, but she didn't have to embarrass George, so I told her to back off. Some of the others heard us. Now she's ...ah...gone, and I feel bad."

I patted her hand. "Don't. It's perfectly normal to defend your husband." And then, because I wanted to change the subject, I asked, "What do you do back home? I know you have a restaurant. Do you both work there?"

Her face brightened. "I work at the restaurant, but I also volunteer at a hospital. I visit patients, bring them magazines, stuff like that. I also have two stepdaughters who spend time with us."

I kept quiet and allowed her to talk. Actually, I enjoyed listening to her speak. She had a soothing, confident voice, like someone doing a commercial for feminine hygiene products. No trace of a regional accent.

"We've both been married before. I don't have any kids." She paused. "I know George doesn't come across as a very pleasant person, but he can be if he tries. Take this trip, for instance. He didn't want to come, but he did it for me."

I stared out the window. We were having a very strange conversation considering the stiffening body in the back of the bus. "Some men are happier staying at home. How about you? Do you like visiting new places?"

I noticed a tiny twitch in the corner of her eye. I couldn't blame her. I was tempted to sit on my hands to stop them from shaking.

"I've traveled a bit. Nothing very exciting."

I was about to ask her more, but Renee scooted into the seat across from us and said, "What are y'all talking about? It's like a funeral where I'm sitting. You'd think someone had died."

"That's not funny, Renee. Can't you see some of us are upset?" I said.

"Oh, lighten up. Why pretend we liked her? Nobody did." She glanced at the body in the back. "Although I suppose that does sound a bit harsh." She leaned in close and whispered, "What do you suppose made her fall? Maybe her husband pushed her."

"Renee!"

Ginger began to visibly shake. She put her hand over her mouth and muttered, "I think I'm going to throw up."

That was enough to make Renee scurry back to her seat. I was tempted to run, too, but that didn't seem very friendly. I thought Ginger was a strange match for loud, brash George, but you never know what attracts people. Maybe they were yin and yang to each other. I had some unfortunate yins in my life before I met Tony, so I knew how seductive a bad yin can be.

We sat in silence for a few minutes. Finally, I said, "How did you meet your husband?" This question was usually a harmless way to make conversation, but to my surprise her face flooded with color.

"I met him at a club. He was the bouncer. I was going through a rough patch—lots of late nights, too much alcohol, that kind of thing. He was nice to me, and I guess one thing led to another and we got married. George's father died and left him the restaurant so we moved to Pittsburgh. You know, for a fresh start. We were looking for happiness."

It sure didn't seem she had found it.

The ride to Vik seemed endless. When we finally arrived and clambered off the bus, we were met by two police cars at the entrance. Four officers escorted us into a small waiting room. Once we were in the building, two men with a gurney removed Lydia's body.

Christof did most of the talking to the authorities. He explained the sudden ash storm, how we briefly lost sight of each other, and how Lydia must have fallen down the precipice. And how Dr. Boucher had examined Lydia and determined what we all knew. She was dead.

The police were cordial. Since they spoke no English and we spoke no Icelandic, the interrogation depended largely on our tour leader's statement. It was easy to see Cameron was distraught and the rest of us were pale and disheveled. At last Christof announced we could get back on the bus and go to the hotel. He waited until we were settled, then stood next to the driver and held onto the back of a seat as the bus careened down the dark road.

"I must inform you," he began, "the authorities will perform an autopsy to determine exactly how Mrs. Cumberland...ah...left us. She will be taken back to Reykjavik. This is required by law. I will have more information for you in the morning, but in the meantime, please have something to eat when we reach our destination. I have informed the hotel we will be arriving late, and they have prepared something for us." He smiled wanly. "And try to rest."

It was after nine o'clock when the bus pulled up to the hotel. As I reached down to pick up my belongings, my hand touched a round metal object. It was silver and the size of a golf ball and much heavier than it looked. I had no idea what it was but I stuck it in my bag, intending to find the owner the next day—and immediately forgot about it.

Most of the group declined dinner, opting instead for bed. Only Ginger and George Reilly and Skip Alessio went into the dark dining room in search of food. They returned a few minutes later, carrying plates loaded with slices of smoked salmon, potatoes and bread. Olivia and I were hungry, and we both wanted a glass of wine to help us relax, but the bar was closed.

"I have a little something in the room," Olivia said. "Why don't we take some of that salmon with us? It looks pretty good."

Why not, indeed.

CHAPTER THREE

Olivia poured wine into two water glasses and handed one to me.

"I knew this would come in handy," she said, indicating the bottle. "I bought it at that little shop when we stopped for a bathroom break." She sank onto her bed and stretched out her long legs. "What a day! I feel so sorry for Cameron. I've never seen a person look so devastated. He must have really loved her, which is more... Nope, I shouldn't say that."

"You mean more than the rest of us did?" I asked. "Go ahead and say it because it's true."

We were only four days into our Iceland trip, but Lydia had already turned out to be someone we tried to avoid. She wasn't batshit crazy like Angela. She was simply arrogant, overbearing and rude. On the very first day when we all gathered for dinner at the hotel in Reykjavik, she made it clear that traveling with a bunch of strangers wasn't her idea of fun. She didn't miss an opportunity to tell us all about her "absolutely first-class" trip to Australia and Mauritius with, of course, only the very best first-class people, which we obviously were not. Cameron had stayed pretty much in the background while his wife shot off her mouth. I had to admit, until she died, I'd hardly noticed him.

"You don't suppose someone got so fed up with her condescending airs, he or she helped her off the precipice?" I laughed when I said it, but Olivia didn't.

"I know I wouldn't have minded pushing her. Others must have felt the same way. I mean who in the world wears a gold lamé raincoat to visit the hot springs? And all that clanging gold jewelry? It was just plain stupid. And in extremely bad taste."

I rolled my eyes, but since she wasn't looking at me, the gesture was wasted. "What I can't figure out," I said, "is why she wasn't wearing the crampons. Christof told us not to walk on the glacier without them."

Olivia reached across the space between the beds and poured more wine into my glass. "You know how she was. She probably decided no one was going to tell her what to do. Maybe she was wearing designer hiking shoes and didn't want to ruin them with crampons."

I offered my friend some salmon. "Still, wouldn't her husband have insisted she keep them on?"

Olivia snorted. "I don't think he could tell her anything. I don't even think he'd try."

I shook my head. "It seems to me, if anyone had seen her without them, someone would have mentioned it." I smeared butter on a hunk of bread and added a slice of salmon.

"Just proves my point. No one cared about her. Considering her abrasive personality, I don't think there's a soul on this trip who'd have dared confront her."

I thought about this. "I'll bet if she ever contemplated her own demise, she never thought it would be on an ash-covered glacier in Iceland. I've been looking at the passenger list. It says here the Cumberlands are from San Francisco. I wonder what he does for a living. And if she worked."

"I think I heard him tell the Sperlings he was in real estate. Actually, Emma might be a good one to talk to. You know how she likes to ferret out information."

This was true. Emma Sperling was a busybody. She pried into the personal lives of anyone who got stuck talking to her.

Olivia got off the bed and put her napkin in the wastebasket. As she went into the bathroom, she said, "Do you notice how everyone in the world is crazy or annoying but us? It really is hard to be perfect, isn't it?"

"Speak for yourself," I said to her retreating back. "I'm not having any problem."

I couldn't think of anyone I'd rather share this experience with than Olivia. My husband, Tony, didn't count because he was beyond conversation now. But in this situation he would have been perfect. He was a cop. He'd risen through the ranks to Captain in Raleigh, North Carolina, and life for us had been pretty good. He'd been on his way home from work and stopped in a convenience store to pick up Advil for me when some idiot decided to rob it. The idiot pointed a gun at the guy behind the counter and demanded money. Tony pulled out his weapon and told him to put his hands up, but the thug turned and fired at my wonderful husband. One bullet and it went right through his heart. He was dead instantly. It still hurt badly every time I thought about it.

Olivia had been my best friend since childhood. We'd gone through a lot together. I loved her no-nonsense personality and her willingness to dive head first into life. She'd had three husbands—none of whom had left her with any money. The first one was a bus driver. She'd married him because he was the best looking man she'd ever seen. And he had impeccable taste in home furnishings and her clothes. He, himself, dressed like a male model in a magazine. He was her ideal dream man. He was also gay.

Husband number two looked like a gorilla. Olivia acknowledged she might have gone overboard trying to find someone rugged and hetero. He was so hetero, even though he was married to my friend he had a string of girlfriends in spite of the impressive growth of hair on his back and in his ears.

Her third attempt at marriage ended a few months ago. He was a sales rep for a major company and seemed like a perfect husband. Unfortunately, his other family thought so, too. His wife and three kids lived in Garner, North Carolina, and thought he spent every other week on the road selling air filters.

Now Olivia vowed she was through with men forever, which was probably a good idea. She and I were so busy running our little lunchroom, we barely had time for anything else. My two kids lived far away—one in Montana and one in Texas—and Olivia had been so busy divorcing, she hadn't focused on conceiving. We both needed to get away from quiches, cupcakes and North Carolina, so we daringly booked this trip to Iceland. Lark Tours promised *a fun-filled exciting adventure enjoying Iceland's glaciers and rugged beauty. Small groups of no more than fourteen. Singles are welcome.* We were up for an adventure. And rugged beauty and glaciers sounded a lot better than the scorching heat of late summer in the South. We couldn't wait to go.

The next morning there was a message from Christof saying we should all meet in the lobby after breakfast. Since the hotel was small and there weren't many guests, the lobby provided an intimate setting for a meeting. When we were all assembled, Christof greeted us, then said, "Well, this has been a sad and upsetting experience. I have been talking with the people in our company and we are trying to figure out what to do. The authorities are conducting an autopsy and Mrs. Cumberland will not be released until it is completed.

We have two options I would like you to consider. We can go back to Reykjavik, and you can all fly home and we will refund a portion of the trip. Or we can continue on." He looked like he was going to cry. "I realize our hearts are heavy. What are you thinking?"

Silence. Emma was the first to speak. "I, for one, have no idea how to continue after this tragedy. It is unbearable."

"Oh, shut up, Emma. You didn't even know her. None of us did." Heads swiveled, but George Reilly was unapologetic. "Hey, I paid for this trip. I vote we go on. It's inconvenient for me to go home now. I've hired a replacement at the restaurant and it would upset things if I went back."

"Well, you're not the only person on this tour. And I think we should go home. I want to get as far away from this awful thing as possible." Renee Alessio put her arm around her husband's waist. "Don't you agree with me, honey? We need to get out of here."

Skip scratched his head. "Don't know. That seems like kind of a cold thing to do. We would be leaving this poor guy here all by himself." He pointed to Cameron. "I'm assuming he's going to wait for his wife's body to be released. Isn't that right, little buddy?"

This show of sympathy from the Muscle Man surprised me. I cringed, waiting for Cameron to take offense to the 'little buddy" comment. Cameron wasn't that short, but his face was a pale oblong and his sagging shoulders and combed-over strands of gray hair made him look smaller than he was.

Skip's comment surprised his wife, too, because she abruptly pulled away from him. "You mean to tell me you're gonna put him before me? Why would you do that?"

"Come on, honey bunch. He's a sad little man."

Lordy, Skip. Please be quiet.

Dirk stepped in front of us and we instantly stopped talking. The man commanded respect without even trying.

"Listen, folks, let's make this quick and let's try to be considerate. Cameron, what are your thoughts? What do you want to do? Do you want to stay here while they perform the autopsy? I can imagine you might want to."

We practically held our breath waiting for him to answer. When he did, he said, 'I'm not going home without my Lydia. They said it will take about five days and I don't want to sit around a hotel waiting while they"—his voice caught—"examine her body. I can't ask you all to stay in Reykjavik, and I don't want to be alone, so if you all want to go on, I will too." His voice quivered when he spoke, and it broke my heart.

The man looked terrible. He wore the same clothes from yesterday and badly needed a shave. It was hard to look at him and not feel compassion.

"So what's the decision?" Dirk asked. "Do we go on? Let's see a show of hands from those who agree."

One by one the hands went up. Even Renee said yes. The last one was Emma, who made a show of finally acquiescing. It really didn't matter what she wanted to do. She was outvoted.

Olivia said she wasn't hungry and was going back to the room to do her hair, but I was starving so I wandered into the dining room. I looked over the breakfast buffet and selected scrambled eggs, waffles and toast. The hotel provided three tables for our group, so I put my plate down on an unoccupied one and took a cup to the coffee machine. When I returned, Renee and Skip were sitting at the table.

The eggs needed salt. In spite of my doctor's warning about my sodium consumption, I asked Renee to please pass the shaker. As she pushed it across the table, I noticed she had an ugly cut on her right hand.

"That looks like it hurts," I said. "I have some stuff in my room that might make it feel better. I'd be happy to get it for you."

She snatched her hand away and stuck it in her lap. "It's nothing. I cut it on a broken glass in our bedroom."

"Really? It looks sort of like a puncture wound. And it looks deep."

She laughed. "I think I would know how I got it. What's it to you?"

"Nothing. Sorry. I didn't mean to be nosy."

I had a habit of noticing things. It was either bad or good, depending on what I was seeing. Renee was obviously annoyed, and I vowed to keep my thoughts to myself on this trip.

Skip smiled pleasantly. "So what's your story?"

"I don't have much of a story. I'm a widow. I live in North Carolina. Olivia and I own a little lunchroom. I like to play tennis. That's about it."

I couldn't help staring at his plate. It contained enough food to feed the entire room. There was an enormous omelet filled with cheese and mushrooms, at least six pancakes, half a loaf of hot bread, enough bacon to clog his arteries forever, and on the side, a bowl of oatmeal. He slurped some coffee and smeared butter on a thick piece of bread. "That doesn't sound very exciting. What do you do for fun?"

"I've had my moments," I told him. "It hasn't been all cake and quiches. What do you do?"

"Me and Renee own a landscaping company in Ohio. We take care of some mighty important property. I don't personally do any of the work anymore. Hired some Mexicans to do that. I mostly spend my days working out and showing folks how to use fitness equipment, like the machine and free weights. I see you eyeing my food. I require a lot of protein to keep these muscles." We both looked at his flexed right arm. "Renee here is also into fitness. She's not bad for a girl."

His wife smiled tightly. "Why don't you just eat your breakfast, honey? Mrs. Greene isn't interested in this."

"Good grief, please don't call me Mrs. Greene. Call me Julia." I wanted to add I wasn't old enough to be called Mrs. Greene, but of course, I was. Renee seemed to think so, too.

"I was just bein' respectful to an older person."

Oh my! Evidently they didn't teach tact in Georgia. It was true certain parts of my body had succumbed to gravity. My upper thighs had wrinkles rivaling a Shar Pei's. I'd discovered if I pulled the skin up, I could still achieve the taut, sexy legs of my youth. However, you can't walk around that way. People tend to ask, "Why are you holding your groin?"

I was saved from further embarrassment when Ginger appeared and said, "Good morning. Are these seats taken?" She held a plate of cheese and smoked salmon.

Skip bestowed one of his megawatt smiles upon her and said, "They sure are not. Here, sit next to me." Using his foot, he pulled out the chair for her.

"Why does she have to sit there?" Thunderclouds formed on Renee's face. "Maybe she wants to sit next to Mrs. Greene or maybe next to me."

Ginger pushed the chair back in and said, "I don't care where I sit. I just want to eat my breakfast."

Skip patted the chair. "So sit here."

Renee looked like she wanted to stab him with the butter knife. Seven thirty in the morning and we were already at each other's throats. I solved the problem by standing up and saying, "Take my seat, Ginger. I'm finished."

I noticed Nicole and Serge Boucher were at the buffet. As soon as they filled their plates, they headed to another table.

"Guess we're not good enough for them," Renee sniffed . "Her Highness is a snooty bitch."

I had to admit, Nicole didn't have much of a warm and fuzzy personality. She was tall and slim and wore her sleek, dark hair pulled back in a ponytail, but aside from looking chic and fit, neither she nor her husband offered much personal information. We knew Serge was a cardiologist, they lived in Walnut Creek, California, and that was about all.

"Let's go, honey," Renee said to her husband. "I don't feel so hot. I need to go to the room."

I needed to leave, too. Angela Fratello had entered the dining room and was already loudly berating one of the wait staff.

"You should always provide a substitute for sugar. Some of us are very health conscious."

Surely she wasn't talking about herself. She was a big-boned, overweight woman with thin, mousey hair and glasses on a chain around her neck. She wore long skirts, men's shirts, sensible shoes and—heaven help us—a ruana. More than once a corner of the would-be shawl had been caught in the bus door.

Ginger and the Alessios quickly got to their feet and exited the dining room, leaving still-steaming cups of coffee on the table. I wasn't so lucky. Angela's head swiveled in my direction as I tried to creep out of the room.

"Good morning, again, Julia," she boomed. "Why are you stooped like that? Bad back? You should let me give you an adjustment."

I straightened up and squared my shoulders. "No problem with my back. Must be on my way."

"Nonsense." She grabbed my arm and hauled me to the buffet table. "Eat some protein. Look, they have fish oil. And this lovely salami."

Her strong fingers were still clamped around my forearm, making it impossible to escape. "I've already had breakfast," I said. "See you on the bus."

She ran her eyes up and down my body. "You mustn't worry about losing your figure. People our age"—and here she nudged me with her elbow— "shouldn't fight the muffin tops. It's part of growing old. Look at my feet." Reluctantly, I swung my eyes to the aforementioned appendages. "They hurt constantly. And my ankles are swollen."

It was hard to see the scuffed black oxfords due to her poor swollen ankles. The pain had to be excruciating. It would cause anyone to act a little loony, and I was actually ready to sympathize with her, but her next words squashed that impulse.

"It's no wonder Lydia is dead. She had no respect for the inhabitants she couldn't see."

Here we go again! I had to get out of there. "I don't think that's a very helpful thing to say, Angela. We didn't know her well, but she seemed nice enough."

No need to share Olivia's and my opinion of the dead lady.

Angela made a very unladylike sound. "You don't have any idea. You should listen to the trolls when they speak. They are all around here. And they speak the truth."

This was one scary lady. I smiled politely, foot poised for a hasty retreat. However, the iron fingers once again grasped my arm.

"I know things. All you have to do is listen." She leaned in so close to me I could smell garlic salami on her breath, and her voice fell to a whisper. "Lydia's fall wasn't an accident. She was murdered."

Huh? Now she had my full attention. She acted as crazy as the bats in my attic back in North Carolina, but I was the widow of a good policeman. I learned from him to listen when people mentioned murder, no matter how insane it sounded. I grabbed a coffee cup, filled it to the brim and followed her to an empty table. I'd had so much caffeine this morning, just looking at the liquid made my heart pump faster, but I was willing to risk a cardiac event to hear what she meant. I waited while Angela filled her plate with herring and hardboiled eggs and put a napkin in her lap.

"So what do you mean she was murdered?" I asked. "That's a pretty serious thing to say."

She wiped her mouth, but missed tiny pieces of egg yolk trapped in her mustache. "I don't make things up, my dear. I know what I know. Would you like me to prove it?"

"Yes, I guess I would." The woman was clearly unbalanced, but I remembered Tony saying to always listen. You never knew what you might hear. "Go ahead and tell me what you know."

Her eyes looked wild. "Someone in our group killed her. There is an evil one among us. We are riding around with a murderer. Soon we may all be dead." As her voice rose, people turned to look at her. The Bouchers were still here, as well as the Sperlings, who had just entered the dining room. And Skip was back, getting a cup of tea for his wife.

I tried to get her to lower her voice, but that was like telling an elephant not to trumpet. The only thing I could do was to pull her to her feet and coax her into the lobby.

"Please try to be quiet," I said, trying to humor her. "We don't want to share this with the others. It might be dangerous."

She, however, was not easy to deceive. "You don't fool me, Julia. I know you don't believe me. That's too bad. I intend to save myself, and I might be able to save you, too."

"Angela, you're scaring me a little bit. If you have some kind of pertinent information, you should share it with the police, not with any of us."

"Bah. The police wouldn't believe me. They would think I'm just as crazy as you do."

This was probably true, but I had to say, "Not if you really do have something important to say."

"I'm going to keep watching and listening to the trolls when they speak. And soon I will divulge all."

"Please don't say things like that to the rest of the group. It will only make them upset. Talk to me if you discover anything new. Is that a deal?"

I said this because we didn't need Angela spouting her ideas to everyone. The thought of that made me very uncomfortable.

"Catch you later, Julia. I see Cameron over there, and I want to have a word with him."

"Please, Angela? Will you promise not to say anything?"

"As you wish. For now, at least."

I had no way of knowing if she would keep her word, but one thing was sure. It would cause chaos if she didn't.

CHAPTER FOUR

"In spite of yesterday's very sad accident, we're going to try to carry on," Christof said.

At the mention of the word, "accident," Angela swiveled in her seat and looked back at me. While Christof talked, my eyes swung around the bus. Emma had left her seat and was bending over Cameron. Renee and Skip were having a fight. She sat with her back to him and her feet in the aisle. His next words prompted her to angrily pick up her tote bag and stalk to an empty seat.

Serge and Nicole both wore earphones and detached expressions. Ginger Reilly's eyes looked like she'd been crying. Her husband had his arm protectively around her shoulder. Only Dirk seemed to be listening to our tour leader.

"Oh my! Pretend we're deep in conversation," Olivia said. Angela was lumbering down the aisle. She fell into the seat across from us and said, "I've been doing a little research since out last chat. I know all about you, Julia. I know your husband was a detective. You probably know all about murders and such."

I sank down in my seat. "Not really."

"No need to be modest. Especially when a crime has been committed."

I cringed. "Please don't say things like that, Angela. People will hear you."

"I know about you, too, Olivia. You've had quite a few husbands. Did you divorce them all, or did some of them die? I'll bet you have some juicy stories to tell."

"I also have tact, Angela. You should try some."

It seemed Angela Fratello was immune to subtle suggestions. We would have to be blunt.

"Zip it, Angela," I said.

But she was not ready to zip it.

"Did you know Lydia Cumberland had a pile of money? She was Cameron's second wife. Not a particularly attractive woman, but I'm sure if you have that kind of cash, you're attractive no matter what." She sniffed. "I've always been happy knowing people like me for who I am."

I hated myself for listening to her, but I had to ask. "How do you know this stuff?"

"Emma told me. Perhaps we should ask her." She stood up, gripped the back of the seat and yelled, "Yoo hoo, Emma! Could you please come here for a minute? Julia wants to talk to you."

I slid farther down in my seat. "That really wasn't necessary, Angela. I don't need to know."

Too late. Emma bustled down the aisle, ready for gossip. "What can I do for you?"

"Angela here says you have info about all of us. Is that true?" Olivia asked.

"I do, indeed."

"How did you get this information?"

"Google, my dear. I Googled everyone on the trip. It was very considerate of the tour company to provide a passenger list in advance. Gave us an opportunity to get to know each other before we actually met."

Olivia turned to me. "You're always on the computer. Did you Google this bunch?"

I shook my head. "Never thought of doing it."

"So who else did you look up?" Olivia extracted a box of chocolate cookies from her bag and offered some to Angela and Emma.

Emma shook her head but Angela took three cookies and placed them in her lap. "Well," Emma began, "I couldn't find much about Ginger Reilly, but I did manage to locate a George Reilly on Bryant Street in Pittsburgh. He owns Reilly's Steak and Ale House. The restaurant had some good reviews. Seems it specializes in thick prime cuts of beef and homemade French fries. Couldn't find much about the Alessios, but we can tell what they're like just by looking at them. Rather boring, don't you think? Dr. Boucher wrote some kind of book about the heart. Also boring."

"Anyway," Emma continued, "Lydia was an heiress. It would be interesting to know if they had a prenup. I'm betting no. She probably thought she was lucky to have attracted a man as good-looking as Cameron. A prenup might have scared him away. And she can't seem to keep a husband. I wonder," she said slyly, "what her first one was like."

I could see Olivia's mind working. "Cameron is good-looking? I guess looks are in the eyes of the beholder. To me he's a thin man with grey hair and a pale complexion. His face looks worn out. Makes me think he spent a lot of years living hard."

Emma sniggered. "My dear, here is the best tidbit. Cameron had to declare bankruptcy. He bought lots of property during the real estate boom and lost it all when the bottom fell out." She inhaled deeply. "Wouldn't that give him a motive for murder?"

So Angela had shared her theory. Emma was speaking quietly, but I still looked around to see if anyone was paying attention. As far as I could tell, no one was listening, but I was happy when Christof took the hand mic again and began to talk.

"Today we're going to stroll on the black basalt sand of our beautiful beach. The cliffs to the west are home to puffins—but they aren't there now—and the jagged peaks you see offshore are basalt rock. There's an interesting folk story connected with them. It is said the rocks are former trolls who tried to drag their boats back to shore and were caught in the waves. That's why they're called Troll Rocks."

"Do people here really believe this gobbledygook about trolls and hidden people?" George laughed derisively. "You have to be nuts if you do."

"I think there is good reason for us to believe in them," Christof said carefully. "People have seen them. And we are cautious about where we build. If there's a big rock in the middle of your property, it might be the home of a troll, and perhaps you will change your mind about putting your home there."

As Christof spoke, I looked out the window of the bus. The sand was coal black, the water a deep Prussian blue. It was easy to see why Icelanders believed the rocks were inhabited by trolls. I was accustomed to the rocks on the Carolina or Maine coast, and these were unlike any I'd ever seen. They looked almost supernatural—like huge jagged peaks rising out of the water. One great oblong mass of basalt had a perfect arch in it.

"You all can get out here, but be careful walking. You must climb over many large stones," Christof told us. "Have a nice time. We'll meet back at the bus in forty-five minutes." He was trying hard to keep the atmosphere as normal as possible, but it was obvious we all had yesterday's event on our minds.

Against Christof's advice, Olivia and I took our shoes off and walked across the black sand. She wandered off to collect stones and I kept walking, enjoying the scenery. The rock formations looked like the sandcastles kids make by dripping wet sand on top of wet sand. The beach was rugged, beautiful, overwhelming and isolated. I felt very insignificant as I stood there watching the waves crash on the shore. I caught myself wishing Tony were with me to see this, which made me feel a bit teary, so I jerked my eyes away from the gorgeous scenery and scanned the beach. Where was everyone?

Angela, wearing a floppy hat, long raincoat and boots, walked alone. She looked upward, as if she were conversing with some celestial being.

I nearly jumped out of my socks when a voice next to my ear said, "This sure doesn't look like anything at home, does it?"

Dirk Harrison looked down at me, an amused smile on his face. I felt my own face grow hot. He was actually not bad looking. Tall, a solid build, thick hair graying at the temples. To be absolutely fair, he was downright handsome, but he was on this trip by himself, so there had to be something wrong with him. It wasn't unusual to see single women on trips—after all, there were far more of them than single men—but it did seem strange to see a man as obviously desirable as Dirk by himself. Like I said, there had to be something wrong with him.

I cleared my throat and said, "No, in North Carolina the Atlantic Ocean is much"...I searched for a word, "gentler." Good grief! Did I just say an ocean was gentle? Had I forgotten how to speak English?

The amused look on his face turned into a broad grin. "Yes, this does look more like the Pacific, the ocean I'm used to seeing."

What a dumb conversation. I was about to smile and walk away when he said, "I noticed you've been chatting with Angela. Interesting woman, isn't she?"

I searched his face to see if he was kidding. Angela *wasn't* interesting. She was annoying. "Talking to a rock would be more fun," I told him.

He laughed. "She does have some unique ideas. Still, sometimes she may be making sense and we don't realize it."

I gave him what I hoped was a piercing look. "What do you mean?"

He shrugged. "Just wondered what she's been saying to you."

All kinds of alarms went off in my head. Why would this handsome, nice man care what a whackadoodle was ranting about? Unless he was interested in the unfortunate demise of Lydia Cumberland. Had he overheard our conversation with Angela? I decided to find out—in a very circuitous way, of course.

"You're from California, aren't you?"

"Yes. I live in Sacramento."

If he was disturbed by the abrupt change in topic, he didn't show it. "Did your wife not want to come with you? I can imagine a trip to Iceland isn't for everyone, especially if you're traveling all the way from the west coast."

"You're full of questions, aren't you? No, my wife didn't want to come with me—mostly because I don't have one. Not anymore."

I was dying to ask if he was divorced or widowed, but instead said, "I see. Are you retired? Or still semi-employed?"

I thought I saw his jaw tighten ever so slightly. "I still work. I suppose you want to know what I do?"

I nodded. "It would be helpful. All in the interest of getting to know each other better, of course."

He studied me briefly. "I'm a lawyer. I try criminal cases. I came on this trip by myself because I've always wanted to see Iceland, and I wanted some alone time. Just me and this magnificent natural beauty. I had no idea I was going to meet a very chatty, but nice, lady."

I felt my face flame. "I'm sorry. I really didn't mean to bother you. If you'll excuse me, I'll slink away now."

"Please don't go. I like talking to you. Let's start over. I asked you what Angela has been saying because I did overhear a bit of your conversation on the bus, and she's also talked to me."

Relief flooded through me. I wasn't the only person who knew her wild theory. And he was a lawyer and used to criminals. Perfect! I looked around to make sure we were alone before I said, "Angela thinks Lydia was murdered."

I waited for him to guffaw and tell me how ridiculous that was. To my surprise, he didn't. "Did she say why she thought that?"

"No. Just something about listening to the hidden people and the truth will come out. You don't think there's anything to her idea, do you?"

He looked out at the ocean. "Let's just say there were some suspicious things."

"Like what?" I demanded. "You have to tell me now. You can't say something like that and walk away."

"If I do, you have to promise to keep my thoughts to yourself. Because that's what they are. Just thoughts. I have no proof of anything. And we certainly don't need hysteria on a bus full of people."

I nodded rapidly. "Just tell me."

"Okay. After we brought Lydia up, I went back down to retrieve her sunglasses and hat. We didn't want to leave anything on the glacier. While I was down there, I saw something glinting in the distance. When I went to see what it was, I found her crampons. They were pretty far from her body and couldn't have fallen down the precipice. If I were a betting man, I would bet someone deliberately threw them there.

But that's not all. When we all boarded the bus again after finding Lydia, I helped Cameron collect her belongings from the seat next to him. As I lifted her backpack, a book she'd been reading fell out, and a piece of paper fluttered to the floor. I picked it up, stuck it in my pocket and didn't look at it until later that night. It was a handwritten note and it said, 'You're going to get what you deserve, bitch. Too bad you'll never see who killed you.'" He frowned. "I know this sounds like melodramatic, cheap novel stuff, but in view of the fact that the lady is dead, there may be some merit in the murder theory. The book had a sticker on the front from a Reykjavik airport shop, which means Lydia didn't bring it with her. She must have bought it after we landed, so the person who wrote the note must be on the bus with us."

I gulped. This was terrible. "Are you going to tell the police?"

"Not right now. I think it would be better to wait for the results of the autopsy. Please keep all this to yourself. I don't want to think about how some of the other passengers would react if they thought there was a killer among us."

He didn't name Emma and Angela, but we both knew that's whom he meant.

My mind went into overdrive. "Why would Lydia keep such a note? Wouldn't she show it to her husband or someone? Surely she would if she thought someone was going to kill her. If I got a message like that it would scare me to death."

He shrugged. "Who knows? Maybe she knew who wrote it and was saving it for a later confrontation. Or maybe she thought it was rubbish and was using it for a bookmark."

So many questions that needed answers but we had to stop talking because Olivia was walking rapidly toward us. I intended to tell my best friend all about my conversation with Dirk, but not when he could hear me. I would keep my promise not to tell the others, but I told Olivia everything.

"Isn't this beach the most awesome thing you've ever seen?" My friend pushed her chestnut hair off her face and said, "You're looking pretty awesome, too." She trained her big brown eyes on Dirk and beamed. One thing about Olivia—she wasn't shy. And since she was a pretty attractive woman, most men were flattered. Dirk, however, seemed unaffected by Olivia's charms. He smiled politely and said he had to get back to the bus.

"I'll bet he's gay," Olivia said. "He's way too good-looking to be straight *and single.*"

"Just because he didn't fall for your line? Maybe you're not his type."

She looked at me as if I were crazy. "How could that be? I'm everybody's type."

Lordy! I glanced at my watch and saw it was time to get back on the bus. The Sperlings were already waiting, as were Nicole and Serge. Ginger and George walked slowly down the beach, hand in hand. I saw Renee and Skip sitting on a rock. But where was Angela?

"I suggest we spread out and look for her," Dirk said. "I'm sure she's just forgotten about the time."

Some of the others weren't happy with this plan. "My feet are wet," Renee said. "I'm not going to hunt for her. Let's just wait a few more minutes. I'm sure she's off talking to some hidden person."

"I'll come," Emma offered. "I have a feeling something might have happened to her."

"Why would you say that, Emma?" Dirk fell into step beside her.

"I don't like the atmosphere around here. We need to all get along with each other. And poor Angela is by herself. She has no one to look out for her."

I eyed her curiously. "Aren't we all being nice? I wasn't aware of any unpleasantness."

"The whole aura of this place is wrong. I don't know if I'm going to be able to tolerate it."

"Sorry to hear that." Dirk pointed to the rocks at the edge of the water. "You saw Angela walking that way, Julia. I think we should look there first."

Olivia went with Emma to scout the area behind the bus, I followed Dirk, and George and Skip went in the opposite direction down the beach. I assumed the others decided to stay in the bus. Christof came running after us.

"I'm coming with you. I hope there's nothing wrong with her. We cannot have another problem."

I felt sorry for him. His face looked tense and worried. This was not a good situation for a tour leader. Or his company.

When Dirk started to run, I knew he'd seen something. Christof and I picked up the pace and soon we saw it, too. Angela was standing on the top of a high rock. And the rock was out a significant distance in the water.

"What is it with her and rocks?" I muttered. "How in the world did she get out there? The water must be over her head."

"No," Christof said. "There's a way to reach those rocks without going under water. But she'll already be very wet."

Dirk stood at the edge of the surf and cupped his hands. "Angela! Can you get off the rock and join us?"

Angela had her arms folded across her chest and stood with her legs apart, looking out to sea. She reminded me of the figurehead on the bow of a ship.

"She can't hear us," Christof said. "We'll have to go get her."

Dirk nodded. "I'm afraid if she doesn't see us coming, we'll scare her and she'll fall off. It doesn't look like there's much room to move around up there."

Christof's face was etched with concern. "But if we don't hug the rocks, we'll be under water." He looked at the waves crashing on the shore. "I do not really want to try to swim in that water."

"Me neither," I echoed. "Is there another way to get to her?"

"I'm worried because the tide is coming in. We must do something soon." Christof rubbed his hands together. "I do not understand how she reached the top. She does not look like an agile woman."

Dirk pointed to a rock adjacent to Angela's. "If I could get up there, maybe I could at least make her hear me. I can't imagine how she's going to get down, though. She surely won't be able to walk down. It's too steep."

As we talked, we were aware of the surf slowly rising around our feet. The more we moved back, the farther away Angela appeared to be. In the back of my mind, I wondered if the others were thinking the same thing I was. Did Angela have help getting up there? I tried to push out of my mind any thought of the hidden people lending a hand. That was ridiculous.

"There *is* a way to get to her," Christof said, "but it's narrow and will be slippery. There's a slim piece of basalt that joins the two rocks. It is about half way up. If we can climb the nearest one, we can get to the joining piece and climb up to Angela."

"That sounds terrifying," I said to no one in particular.

Christof smiled. "It really is not. As children we used to hide from each other on those rocks. We all knew how to quickly get from one rock to another. I believe this is the only possibility to get Ms. Fratello down."

"Okay. Julia, Christof and I will go get her. Can you please tell the others where we are? And then perhaps bring a few blankets down here?"

As I turned to go, Nathan Sperling came running across the sand. "Christof, you have to come back to the bus," he gasped when he stopped puffing from the exertion. "Some of the ladies are insisting the driver take them back to the hotel. They say they're too cold and tired to sit around waiting for Angela. The driver speaks enough English to understand what they want, and he refuses to move. You have to calm things down."

"But I have to get out to the rock. Is it not possible for you to handle this?" Our tour leader looked distressed.

"I'm not getting involved in this. One of the ladies is my wife. Come now. I think this is your job. Aren't you responsible for this group?"

I was about to protest loudly about such an uncalled for remark when Dirk put a hand on my arm and said, "Go ahead, Christof. We'll be fine. I have the indomitable Ms. Greene with me. Just tell us how to get to the connecting piece."

Undecided, Christof looked at us and back at the bus. Finally he said, "Go to the east side of the first rock and towards the front. You must climb it. Unfortunately, you will get wet. You will find natural handholds, almost as if the hidden people built it for themselves," he said with a grin. "The connector is halfway up. Be careful on it because it is quite narrow. The path on the next rock goes around in a spiral. You will see it." As if to reassure us, he added, "Remember, we played on this as children. It holds no fear for us."

That was peachy. I didn't know about Dirk, but I couldn't say the same for me.

CHAPTER FIVE

The water was above my knees. And cold. The swells threatened to wash over my chest, but the east side of the rock was more protected from the turbulent sea. I was wet and scared, but the waves weren't bashing against me. I hung onto Dirk's hand and briefly regretted coming with him. Or coming to Iceland, for that matter. I should have stayed in dull but wave-free Wake Forest.

As if reading my thoughts, he said, "Maybe you should go back. I can do this alone. And the others are sure to come soon to help."

"I'll bet they don't. I think it's you and me, babe. I'm coming with you in case Angela insists she isn't going anywhere with a man. Or in case she tries to throw you off the rock."

He squeezed my hand, and we plunged onward. Up close, the enormous rock towered over our heads, and we could no longer see the flat top.

"It shouldn't be long, now," Dirk said. "Christof said we'd see natural hand-holds. Are you sure you can do this?"

"Let's put it this way. I ain't going back by myself. Besides, Angela got up there, and I'm going to bet I'm in better physical shape than she is. It must be easier than it looks. What I'm wondering is—how are we going to get out of here? The tide will really be in, and the water will be over our heads."

"Worry about that later. Here, this is something to wrap your hand around. It must be what Christof meant."

He grabbed pieces of rock that jutted out like a tree limb, took hold of another and hand over hand, hauled himself up.

"I'll be darned. There is a path of sorts. Come on, it's not that hard to do."

Maybe not for him, but my hands were cold and wet and the rock handholds were difficult to hang on to. I tried to pull myself up, but my arms felt like they were going to drop off. I should have done more upper body workouts at the gym, but this was no time for remorse. I didn't intend to lose sight of Dirk, so I had to get going.

I don't know how I got as far as I did, but when I felt strong hands grab my arms and effortlessly drag me to the path, I almost collapsed in relief.

"This is amazing," Dirk said. "It's obvious people have used this route for a long time. See how worn the rock is? Many feet have traveled this way."

"Great. Where's the connecting thingy? Let's find it and get off here."

But Dirk was having fun. "You don't see any of this from the shore. From back there this rock looks like a forbidding mass of basalt. I wonder what people have done up here."

"You're not going to start with the trolls and hidden people, are you?"

"No, but I can understand how the Icelanders think they may exist. This country is beautiful, rugged, intimidating, and vastly different than anything in the United States. The sheer majesty and fierceness of nature kind of overwhelms me here."

Lordy! "I'd love to have this discussion with you some other time. Perhaps over a nice glass of wine in front of a roaring fire, but right now I want to get Angela."

He pointed to a bridge-like piece of basalt about two feet wide. "There it is. We're going to have to be sure-footed to get across."

"You go first," I told him, "and I'll hold onto your jacket. So don't fall."

I closed my eyes, and taking baby steps, minced across.

"Christof sure knew what he was talking about," Dirk said. "The basalt path does seem to twist around the rock. Amazing! We wouldn't exactly call this a walking trail in America, but it sure is coming in handy here."

Soon we were high enough to see Angela's feet and legs. "I don't want to alarm her," Dirk whispered. "Maybe we should sneeze or cough or something."

I obliged by blowing my nose loudly on a tissue I found in my pocket.

"Who's there? Have you come back to show me the way?"

Good. She heard us. We could figure out whom she was talking about later.

"Angela, we've come to help you down. It's time to get back on the bus." Dirk's voice was authoritative enough to make me jump, so I figured Angela must be on her way.

Instead we heard, "Who are you?"

"Dirk. Dirk Harrison. Will you join us now?"

"I don't know you. Besides I'm waiting for someone."

His lips tightened into a straight line. "Angela, you *do* know me. We've been traveling together for several days. Let's go. The bus won't wait much longer."

"Go away."

This was, indeed, a conundrum. We couldn't stay where we were much longer, and she refused to come with us.

"Let me try," I said softly to Dirk. In a loud voice I called, "Angela, it's me, Julia. We were worried about you, so we came to find you. You must have a wonderful story to tell. How about coming down and sharing it with us?"

Silence.

"Angela? Let's go back to the hotel and have a cup of tea. Okay?"

"I'm afraid I don't know how to get down. You can come up here, but he can't."

Dismayed, I looked at Dirk. "How do I do that? What if I can't find the right way?"

"It looks fairly simple," he said. "I'll come with you as far as I can without her noticing me. Once you bring her down, we can both deal with her."

That sounded ominous, but we didn't have time to stand around chatting. I followed Dirk until he motioned for me to go ahead. I clung to the rock wall and inched my way up. I neglected to mention that I was terrified of heights. Just peeking over a high place gave me vertigo and the urge to hurl myself off. When I reached Angela, I tried to focus my eyes on her because I knew if I looked down, I was done.

Angela, however, had no such problem. "The view is lovely from up here, Julia."

"I'm sure it is, but we have to go now. The others are waiting. Cameron needs to get back to the hotel."

"Of course. I don't want to be thoughtless. And I don't want that man to suffer anymore. Not after what he's endured."

She sounded normal and aside from being soaking wet to her knees, looked pretty good, too. But clearly, Angela had bats flying around her belfry. I was very glad Dirk was waiting for us. I took her hand and led her around the rock. She seemed passive until Dirk appeared and said, "Hi, Angela. I'm happy you decided to come down."

"You!"

She shrank back against me as if she'd seen something terrible. Angela is a strong woman—I remembered how her fingers had gripped my arm in the restaurant—but now she cowered like a frightened child. I looked helplessly at Dirk as he tried to escort her to the connector.

"Don't touch me!" she shrieked. "You can't be here. You know you can't."

Tiny prickles of fear began to run through my body. Angela was genuinely afraid of Dirk. But why? Was she mistaking him for someone else? She surely knew who he was. She had ridden in the bus with him for four days and had never reacted this way. Now she and I were alone with him on this rock. What if he turned out to be a bad guy? One gentle nudge and we could both be shark food.

"I don't mean to upset you, Angela. I just want to see you safely on the beach. Can we please go down?"

She had no choice. We couldn't stay up there forever. I took her hand and said to Dirk, "You go ahead. We'll follow you."

"Maybe you should go first. I can bring up the rear and make sure nothing happens to you."

"Nope, we'll be fine. After you," I told him.

He gave me a peculiar look but didn't argue. We reached the connector and the other rock without incident. When we approached the place where we'd begun our ascent, Christof was waiting in a zodiac to take us to shore. Relief flooded his face.

"I've been watching you with binoculars. Well done. The water is too deep now to wade through, so I borrowed this boat from the people in the hotel. I'm afraid our group is not very happy," he said as he started the motor. "It will be good when we get to our room and warm clothes. We were supposed to reach Selfoss tonight, but I've arranged for us to go back to Vik. The ride to Selfoss would take too long."

Christof was the only one who spoke on the short ride to the hotel. We were all immersed in our own thoughts, and mine were confused and disturbing.

CHAPTER SIX

"I sure don't ever want to do that again. I have no idea what scared Angela so badly about Dirk, but I was afraid we weren't going to be able to get her down."

Olivia and I sat in the warm bar of the hotel. I felt human again after a long hot shower. We both ordered Icelandic vodka on the rocks, which seemed like an appropriate beverage for this evening. So far, we were the only ones from our group enjoying a pre-dinner cocktail.

"Well, it was no picnic on the bus, either," Olivia said. "After Emma and I struck out hunting for Angela, we came back to find Renee having a fit. She said she was cold and tired and demanded to be driven to the hotel, but the driver refused. Then the little lady let loose a string of profanities that would have made a sailor blush, which I'm pretty sure the driver, happily, didn't understand. Although it was easy to get the gist of her remarks from the vein that bulged in her forehead.

It got nasty when Emma joined the whine fest. She kept insisting she had to get to the hotel so she could take her pills. That woman has a voice that could shatter glass. When I suggested—and calmly, I might add—that she simply open her luggage, remove the required medication and swallow them right there on the bus, she clutched her chest and said she was having heart pains. Her sappy husband helped lower her to a seat and stood next to her, fanning her face. He is powerless to control his wife. He sort of fades into the background when she starts yammering."

"I wish I'd had a chance to talk to Angela by herself," I said, "but as soon as we got on the bus, we were surrounded by angry people, and she clammed up and refused to say a word. I have to know how she got up on that rock. Want to know what I think?"

Olivia stirred her drink with her finger. "I know you're about to tell me."

"I think someone who's very familiar with the Troll Rocks led her up there."

My friend considered this. "But who would that be? To the best of my knowledge, no one on the tour has ever been to Iceland. Remember our first night in Reykjavik at our introductory dinner? Christof asked if anyone had ever visited Iceland before this trip and no one raised his or her hand. Maybe Angela managed to stumble up there by herself."

I shook my head. "Not a chance. You have to have seen it, Olivia. If you didn't know precisely where to step and hold on, you would never make it. And I'll tell you something else. Whoever led her up there meant to leave her there. She could easily have fallen off. And for sure she didn't know how to get down."

"But who would want to hurt Angela? She's several bricks shy of a load, but she isn't dangerous."

"What if she's right about Lydia being murdered? And the murderer doesn't like her running around telling everyone."

Olivia and I were so engrossed in our conversation, we didn't see George and Ginger Reilly until George cleared his throat and said, "Can we buy you two a drink?"

Olivia shot me a look that said, *Uh oh. How much did they hear?* "Sure," she replied. "I'll never turn down this excellent vodka."

Ginger and George settled into chairs next to us and for a few minutes we tried to navigate through awkward conversation. I agreed with Ginger that the wood-paneled walls and lace curtains gave this place "a real rustic look."

George ordered a beer and his wife a glass of white wine. Ginger looked fragile this evening. Her white skin was almost translucent and makeup failed to hide the dark circles under her eyes.

"What's your impression of Iceland?" Olivia asked. "It's a beautiful country, isn't it?"

Ginger shrugged her shoulders. "It's too barren for me. There are never any people walking around. And there are no places to shop."

This was true. Iceland was certainly not a shopper's paradise. Outside of Reykjavik, we saw very few houses and stores. But the countryside in the south was gorgeous—lush green fields, soaring mountains, volcanoes and the occasional house with a blue or red roof.

"We didn't come here to shop though, did we? I mean where else in the world can you see scenery like this?" I asked.

George didn't want to talk about scenery. "So what do you make of this whole business with Angela? What was she doing on the rock?"

"I honestly don't know," I told him. "We didn't have a chance to talk."

George frowned. "I heard her say she thought Mrs. Cumberland was murdered."

I tried to keep my expression neutral. "Really? Well, you know she has a vivid imagination and is intensely interested in all the Icelandic folklore. She may be confusing things in her mind. You probably shouldn't pay too much attention to what she says."

George drained his glass and ordered another. "That's interesting you'd say that since I happen to know she talked to you."

"And I just told you I don't believe much of what she says."

"But what if she *was* murdered? That would make one of us a killer."

Olivia interrupted. "This kind of speculation is pure nonsense. Why would anyone on this trip do something like that? What would be the motive? We didn't know each other before a few days ago."

"I told you to stop telling people that, George. It gives me the creeps. Can't we talk about something else?" Ginger's hand shook as she picked up her glass of wine.

Dirk Harrison came into the bar, nodded in our direction and took a seat by himself. Olivia raised her eyebrows questioningly at me. I didn't know what I felt about him now. Before we rescued Angela, I'd have bet he was an honest, trustworthy, genuinely nice man. But her reaction to him changed everything. The camaraderie he and I felt on the way up the rock was gone.

"Tell me about your restaurant," Olivia said to Ginger. "Is it a big place?"

Relieved to be talking about something else, Ginger said, "We have twenty tables and a bar. It's upscale. White tablecloths and such. People have to call in advance for reservations and we have plenty of out-of-town guests. I'm excited about putting in a real dessert cart that the server can wheel to the tables."

"That's a crappy idea. Let them order from the menu. You're always trying to change the place. Stay home where you women belong and let me run the business. It's a bar and grill, and it's going to stay that way."

Embarrassed for her, I ignored George's glares and said, "That sounds lovely. I'm sure it would be a great addition."

He threw a handful of nuts into his mouth and said, "So are you an expert in the restaurant business?"

"No, I'm not," I snapped, "but I do know a little bit about serving food in a pleasant atmosphere. I'm sure your wife's sweet personality is one of the reasons you've been successful. And, by the way, women no longer stay home barefoot in the kitchen. Many of us actually work."

"That's rich. You don't know what you're talking about, does she, sweetheart?" He patted his wife's cheek. "Does your sparkling personality help the restaurant?"

Ginger turned the color of a beet and pulled away from him. "Leave me alone. You've had too much to drink."

This man was a jerk. I felt sorry for his wife so I quickly tried to change the subject. "Wasn't the black beach beautiful? And I've never seen such deep blue water."

Christof walked into the bar and motioned to us. "If you would please come now. Dinner is ready."

Thank heavens!

Angela didn't come to dinner. Christof said she had a bad headache and had ordered soup sent to her room. After an excellent meal of arctic char, new potatoes and fresh green beans, Olivia and I said goodnight and headed to our room. As we passed the reception desk, I stopped to ask for Angela's room number.

"I intend to knock on her door and ask if she'd like some Advil, so I have to stop in our bathroom first and retrieve mine," I said. "I know I shouldn't intrude, but it's killing me not knowing why she was so scared."

"I'll be interested to hear what you learn," Olivia said. "Don't stay too long or I'll worry the hidden people have snatched you."

I hurried into our room and into the bathroom to retrieve the bottle of pills. When I didn't find it there, I remembered I'd stuck it in my tote bag. I quickly emptied the contents on my bed and searched for the plastic bottle. The little silver ball I'd found on the floor of the bus rolled into my hand. I'd completely forgotten about it. I examined it more closely and saw the initials *LMB* and the words *with all my love* engraved around the middle. Who had a last name beginning with B? Nicole Boucher. Maybe it belonged to her. I intended to ask when I saw her.

I grabbed the Advil and walked down the hall to Angela's room. I stopped in front of her door, took a deep breath and tapped lightly. When the door swung open, I expected to see Angela, so I stepped back in surprise when Nicole Boucher said, "Hi. I was checking on her. Guess we both had the same idea."

The room was dark except for a dim light coming from the bathroom.

"She's asleep now, poor thing. I brought something for her nerves."

I tried to peer around Nicole, but she blocked the door.

"What did you give her? Whatever it was must have worked fast."

"I have some Xanax, but she hasn't taken it yet. My husband thought it would be a good idea because she seemed so upset on the way back to the hotel, but she was asleep when I got here."

"I'll just leave the Advil for her because Christof said she had a bad headache." Nicole couldn't very well deny me entrance. She stepped aside and I quickly moved into the room. The soup Angela had ordered was untouched. Her glasses and a map of south Iceland were on the bed. As far as I could tell, she'd only partially undressed. Her wet skirt hung over a chair, but she was still wearing the brown shirt I'd seen her in this afternoon. And I didn't see her shoes anywhere. Surely she wasn't wearing them in bed. I went into the bathroom to fill a glass of water for her, and quickly searched the floor for the wet oxfords. They were in the tub.

Nicole stood at the open door, obviously waiting for me to leave, so I placed the Advil on the table where Angela was sure to see it and took another quick look around the room. Something felt off. Why wasn't she completely undressed? And why did she order soup if she didn't intend to eat it? Was her headache so severe that she couldn't even swallow liquid?

I couldn't linger any longer so I brushed past Nicole, and she gently closed the door behind us. It surprised me that she was so concerned about one of our fellow travelers. Since she and her husband had kept to themselves so much, the gesture seemed out of character.

"I'm glad to see you," I said as we walked down the hall together. "Are you perhaps missing a small silver ball? It's fairly heavy, so it probably isn't meant to be worn. I found it on the floor of the bus. It is engraved with the letter B."

She shook her head. "I don't wear much jewelry, and that doesn't sound like something I would own. Sorry."

"No problem. I happened to see it just now and thought I'd ask. By the way, I'm sort of curious. If Angela was asleep when you came, how did you get into her room?"

"The door wasn't locked. I knocked and when she didn't answer, I tried the knob. I went in because I was worried she might not be okay. But she seemed to be sleeping peacefully. I checked her pulse and it was slow and regular."

It was the longest speech I'd ever heard Nicole make. I supposed what she said was perfectly logical, but as I said goodnight and entered my room, I wondered why I felt like something sinister was going on. Olivia had already fallen asleep, so I couldn't rely on her to tell me I was being silly. As I brushed my teeth and got ready for bed, I tried to shake it off. I was getting as whacky as Angela.

CHAPTER SEVEN

The next morning I caught up with Angela outside the hotel as we waited for the bus. She looked pale and subdued, but I was happy to see she was wearing a different shirt and skirt this morning.

"You had me worried," I told her. "What on earth scared you so badly? Was it Dirk? And how did you get to the top of that rock? I know I'm being extremely nosy, but I'm dying to know."

Her face closed. "I don't want to talk about it."

"But why not, Angela? I'm genuinely concerned about what's upsetting you."

"They told me not to say anything." She clutched her tote bag to her chest and clamped her mouth shut. "Someone drugged me last night. I fell asleep before I could... I think it must have been...well...you know who. They were worried about what I would say."

"Who drugged you? Someone from our group?"

"I'm not going to tell. You don't believe in them, anyway, so what would be the point?"

"Do you mean the hidden people? Did you see them? Angela, that would be very exciting. If you say you did, I'll believe you."

When she didn't answer, I said, "If you know where they live, I'd love to go with you to visit them." As I spoke those words, I realized that was the truth. If the hidden people were responsible for Angela's trek up the rock, I wanted to meet them.

"I don't know if they'd like that," she said cautiously. "I suppose I could ask."

"That would be wonderful. Could we try now?" I was willing to miss whatever outing Christof had planned.

Emma Sperling picked that precise moment to come over to us and say, "I've made printouts for everyone of Christof's remarks about the beach at Vik. I thought you might like a copy. As you can see, I've also included colored maps and have drawn pictures of objects of interest."

She handed me four or five pages of paper stapled together. The small, pinched writing made my eyes water.

"This is very kind, Emma, but I think I'm up on things. I've been listening and taking photos."

"Really? I noticed you have either been dozing or chatting in the back of the bus. I stayed up late transcribing this for you."

"Then I'll certainly enjoy it. Thank you."

I waited for her to move away, but she also had something to say to Angela. "You poor dear. You look like you could use some of my herbal potion. It would make you feel wonderful. I have some in my bag."

Angela shot me a dismayed glance. "No, thank you. I feel fine."

I wondered what was in Emma's "potion." She was noticeably happier after a swig from one of her bottles.

The bus pulled up in front of the hotel and one by one we boarded and took our seats. I waited, hoping Angela and I could sneak away, but Christof came running out of the hotel and yelled at us to get onboard. So I lost my chance to have what promised to be an enlightening discussion with Angela and her hidden friends.

"Hello, folks. Was not our black beach fantastic? I know most of the sand in America is white, so this was something special. As some of you know, many of our homes are heated by geothermal energy. Today I am going to show you some examples of that. And then we will do something very exciting. We will visit swimming holes hidden under massive rocks."

Emma immediately put her reading glasses on her nose and opened a notebook. I sighed as I saw her raise her hand.

"Could you explain the process of geothermal energy? It must be a very complicated procedure."

Several people groaned. George Reilly yelled, "Put a cork in it, Emma. Read a book or something."

Christof diffused the situation by saying, "We will visit a geothermal power plant later today. Perhaps we can save the explanation for then?"

"That's something I won't be doing," Olivia said. "Maybe there will be some shops."

I glanced out the window at the scenery rushing by. There were mountains and vast expanses of green and the occasional house, but I hadn't seen a shop for five days.

"Better think up something else to do," I told my friend. "I don't think you're going to be able to spend your krona."

The bus stopped next to a deep crater, its walls made of rock. It was filled with lovely deep blue water. The doors to the bus swung open and Christof said, "Follow me, please. I will show you some interesting things."

He led us to a place where steam shot out of the ground. "This is how we heat our homes. This is a hot spring. We harness this energy. It is very clean. You may have noticed Iceland has no pollution."

Renee adjusted her sunglasses and folded her arms. "This is super boring," she said in a whisper. "I don't care how they heat their houses."

I sort of agreed with her. I had way too much swirling around in my mind to focus on geothermal energy. The rest of the group seemed to feel the same way because no one was paying particular attention— except Emma, who was scribbling furiously in her notebook. As I looked around at the others, I saw Cameron had found a buddy. Nathan Sperling sat next to him on the bus and now stood with him, talking quietly. I wondered if he'd heard anything from the police in Reykjavik about his wife's autopsy. He looked healthier than he had in the hours immediately after Lydia's death. His color was better, and as I watched, I saw him smile at something Nathan said.

Christof finished his little lecture about hot springs and said, "Now I am going to show you one of my favorite swimming places. You will see why I asked you to wear your bathing suits under your clothes."

I didn't see anything that resembled a swimming pool, but apparently Renee did. She peeled off tight jeans and shrugged out of her lavender jacket.

"My, my," Olivia said. "Aren't you cold?"

Renee wore a teeny pink bikini bottom and top, which had quite an effect on the men. Even Nathan Sperling gaped, slack-jawed, at her.

"Remind me to start going to the gym when we get home," I said to Olivia. "It obviously pays to work out."

We followed Christof until we stood in front of a massive rock that was humped like a whale. At the bottom were two jagged openings.

"Here we are. This is where I went swimming as a teenager. The water below is warm because it is heated by our famous thermal springs. One of these openings was for boys and one for girls." He smiled. "But once you are in the water, they are connected. We had great fun."

I walked to one of the openings and looked down. About six feet below I could see black water.

"Do you want to try it?" Christof asked. See the indentations in the rock? Use them as steps."

I shook my head. I get claustrophobia in an elevator, so I was pretty sure being six feet underground would make me stop breathing. Renee, however, pranced to the opening, stuck her perky little derriere into the air as she located the steps, turned around and lowered herself into the water.

Ginger and George walked to the edge of the boy's opening. George was already stepping out of his pants.

"I'll be back in a minute," he said. "Just want to see what this is all about."

"Please don't do that, George," Ginger said. "It doesn't look safe."

I could have predicted her husband would pay no attention to her. As he descended into the water, Ginger turned to me. "I hate this trip. I wish we hadn't come."

"It's not that bad." My reply was automatic, but I sort of agreed with her.

Olivia took a step towards the opening, peered down and backed away. "They have to be nuts. You won't catch me going down there."

The others in the group eventually wandered away. Emma and Nathan walked with their heads bowed, intent on reading their guidebooks. Cameron and Dirk leaned against the bus and chatted. In spite of my misgivings about Dirk, I thought it was good Cameron had someone smart and sensible to talk to. Dirk may have done something that had terrified Angela, but he was still an intelligent man. Angela had stayed on the bus. I didn't see Serge or Skip. Olivia was talking to Nicole about shopping in San Francisco.

Apparently no one was fascinated or worried about our companions down in the water. I meandered over to the edge of the boy's opening and bent down to look in. I remember thinking it was strange I couldn't hear voices. Surely sounds would echo from the underground chamber. I straightened up, intending to tell Christof I was concerned about our friends.

Instead of standing upright, I fell forward, arms flailing, into the dark water. Afterwards, the others told me I must have lost my balance. But I knew I didn't. I felt a hand on my back and a definite shove.

CHAPTER EIGHT

Incongruously, my first thought as I sank beneath the surface was *Come on! Really?* And my second was that Christof was right. The water was warm. My jeans, jacket and walking shoes weighed me down and made effective swimming impossible. Not that I could ever swim effectively even in a Speedo and goggles. Swimming was right up there with conquering high places—something I couldn't do very well. So when panic threatened to overwhelm me, I kicked and prayed and kicked and prayed and held my breath. It seemed to be taking an awfully long time to come back up.

When at last my head broke out of the water, I was exhausted. And terrified. I tried to scream, but when I opened my mouth, I swallowed water. Now I imagined I was drowning. I tried to calm myself by remembering how Olivia and I went swimming last summer. At least that's what we called it. I moved back and forth in the pool by pulling myself forward with my arms and letting my legs float behind me. I'd told her I was strengthening my upper body.

So do it now, I urged myself. Above me I could see the opening in the rock. If I could get over to it, I could climb out. Piece of cake. It should be very simple.

But it wasn't. The footholds in the rock were slimy and I couldn't get a grip. Every time I tried, my hands slipped off. And where were the others? Christof said the two openings connected, but I didn't hear any voices. When my hand finally touched a rock that wasn't slippery, I held on for dear life.

"Help!" I yelled, making sure my face was out of the water. Someone up there had to hear me. "Hey! Anybody! Help!" I somehow expected an echo, but there was none. In fact, the sound of the underground spring was so loud, I could barely hear my own voice, so it was possible the others were swimming and laughing on the other side.

What to do? I couldn't attempt to swim over there encumbered as I was by so many clothes. Reluctantly, I shrugged out of my jacket and watched it float away. I felt lighter but still not ready for a plunge into the darkness. I tried yelling again. Someone must have missed me by now. Where was Olivia? Surely when she didn't see me anywhere near the group, she would deduce something awful had happened and immediately think of the openings in the rock. But there was no response from up above. And maybe I was giving Olivia too much credit. She was probably sitting somewhere enjoying a glass of wine.

I decided to take off my jeans because doing this would allow me to kick better. I held onto the piece of jagged rock, unzipped them and let them slide down my legs. Slight snag in my plan. I couldn't get the jeans off because my shoes were in the way, and I couldn't pull them back up because they were filled with water.

Real panic clawed at my chest. I was going to drown in this black hole and when someone found me—if anyone ever did—I would have my pants down around my ankles. I could already see them pointing and guffawing.

I couldn't move and my hand that gripped the rock was falling asleep, and the hot water was making me feel sick. And tired. Very, very tired. It was no wonder folks weren't supposed to stay in these hot springs for very long. It would have been hot in Renee's teensy bikini but fully dressed it was unbearable.

What a way to end my life, I thought. This would really amuse Tony. Maybe it wouldn't be so bad. It was nice and warm, and I would slip under the water, and that would be it.

When round bright circles played on the surface, I thought I was already seeing the entrance to the Other Side. It was strange, though. I always figured it would be a brilliant beam of multi colors, not errant flashes darting across the black water.

A burst of light hit me in the face, and I screamed, "Jesus, is that you?"

"Julia? Is that you?"

I imagined I could faintly hear Olivia's panicked voice. What was she doing here? Were we going to the Great Beyond together? Before I knew what was happening, someone was next to me, and a strong hand grabbed my arm.

"I'll pull you to the other entrance," Dirk said. "We can't get up here."

"No kidding." Apparently the fear of imminent drowning hadn't stifled my snarky side. As soon as I realized a real person had come to save me and was not some ethereal being from Way Beyond, I recovered quickly. I started to release my hold on the rock so I could go with him, but then remembered my pants—the ones that had now fallen around my shoes. If I could just use two hands, I could probably pull them back up.

"If you can get me to the other side, though, I will be most grateful." I sounded like Mary Poppins, but I didn't care. I was terrified and absolutely wanted to be rescued, but wasn't sure my savior wasn't a bad guy who intended to push me under water and finish the job.

Dirk, however, didn't seem to notice my mental state. Saying nothing, he easily hauled me through the water. As I looked up, I saw faces clustered around the opening.

"You go first," he said. "I'll follow to make sure you don't slip."

"Nope."

"Excuse me?"

"I can't go first. I have my reasons."

"Would you like to tell me what they are? You may not have noticed, but I jumped into this hole fully dressed. I'd really like to climb out now and dry off."

"Julia," Olivia called. "What's the problem? Are you hurt? If not, get up here."

Dirk tried to move me forward. "You heard the lady. Move."

"Listen," I said urgently, "don't ask any questions, but I need to pull my pants up. I tried to take them off so I could swim, but they wouldn't slide over my shoes. I need both hands to fix them, so if you could keep me upright while I pull, I would really appreciate it."

Through the faint light coming from above, I saw Dirk smile. "I'll do it for you."

"I don't think so."

"Okay. Have it your way. Do you want to climb out with your jeans around your feet or should I help you. We're not teenagers, you know. I can promise you I've felt a woman's ass before."

"I don't think it will be necessary for you to feel mine," I said, "but perhaps it would be okay for you to help me."

Without saying another word, he reached around me, took hold of my pants and yanked them to my waist. And he didn't touch my ass.

"Thank you."

"No problem. After you."

By stepping on the jutting rocks and grabbing them with my hands, I managed to haul myself to safety. As my eyes met the bright glare of sunlight, I felt like a bat emerging from a cave. A chorus of voices greeted me.

"What happened? Did you get dizzy and fall? Why were you standing so close to the edge of the hole?"

I waved them away. "Is there somewhere I could go to dry off?" I asked Christof.

"Right up there." He pointed to a small restaurant. "I have planned to have coffee served for all the swimmers."

I dragged Olivia with me and didn't speak until we were in the ladies room. She handed me a wad of paper towels.

"What on earth made you jump in? That was pretty stupid."

I stepped out of the soggy jeans and swiped ineffectively at my legs. "I didn't jump. And I didn't fall. You're going to think I'm crazy, but I distinctly felt someone shove me."

My friend looked doubtful. "You know, Julia, you're getting to that age where your balance might be…well…a bit compromised. I can understand if you don't want to admit it."

"There's nothing wrong with my balance," I snapped. "I'm not making this up. I felt someone push me."

"But why would someone do that?" she asked. "It doesn't make sense. I hope you're not getting caught up in all the myths and folklore nonsense." She opened her bag and pulled out a pair of tights and a blue, cowl neck sweater. "You can wear these. I keep them for emergencies." She eyed me critically. "Not exactly your style, but they're dry."

Since it was either wear them or run around in my soaking wet Jockey panties, I gratefully thanked her. The tights accented an already ample backside, but if I pulled the sweater low enough, I could cover at least part.

As I applied more lipstick and ran a comb through my wet hair, I said, "Did you see anyone near the opening in the hole?"

She shook her head. "I was talking to Nicole. She really is a nice person. Quite intelligent. Did you know she and her husband breed English cocker spaniels? Just as a hobby, but one of the females has quite an impressive bloodline. I was thinking…"

"Olivia! Focus. Someone pushed me into the water. Who could it have been?"

"I don't know. I wasn't paying attention to the rest of the group. I think I saw Ginger and George walking together, but maybe not. Maybe that was yesterday. I think George went swimming." She blushed slightly. "I did at some point notice you weren't anywhere around. I must have had a worried look on my face because Dirk saw me and asked what was wrong. I didn't think you could be in the water," she said defensively. "You don't like to swim. And what kind of idiot jumps—fully dressed—into a swimming hole? I hunted all over the place for you. But not there."

We stopped talking as Angela came into the bathroom. She ran her eyes over my body and said, "Bad things happen to bad people. You are paying for being unfriendly and mocking."

"Hey! I thought we were friends. And I have to tell you I'm not an unfriendly person. You can ask anyone. Just because I'm not into your elves and trolls doesn't mean I'm mocking you. You're free to believe whatever you wish. And so am I."

I flounced to the door, Olivia right behind me.

"So I guess you don't want to hear who pushed you into the water."

I stopped so suddenly, Olivia slammed into my back. "Angela, do you really know? This is wonderful. Well, it's not wonderful I was shoved down the hole, but you know what I mean. My friend here doesn't believe me. Do you know who did it?"

Angela nodded vigorously. "Indeed I do. Too bad we're not friends."

Angela was clearly not mentally stable, and for the hundredth time I wondered if she was a danger to herself or anyone else on the trip. I felt I had to treat her as if she were a small child.

"But we are friends. I really do like you. So please tell me who did it. Was it Emma Sperling?"

She recoiled in horror. "Certainly not. Emma is a lovely woman. So talented. She crochets beautifully. She is making a tam for my little niece."

"A what?"

"A tam-o-shanter. A little hat. Don't you know anything?"

I brushed aside her praise of Emma's crocheting skills. "So who did you see, Angela? This is serious business. Someone tried to hurt me. You saw it yourself."

"It's your fault, you know. They know you don't believe in them."

I heard Olivia say, "Uh oh."

"You did see an actual person, didn't you? You said you saw someone push me. That has to mean a real flesh-and-blood individual."

Angela didn't appear to be listening. "At first, I thought it might be a troll wife. They're nasty creatures. You don't want to mess with them. But then I realized it was probably an elf." Her face scrunched into a frown. "They let you see them if they want to. They're not always hidden, you know."

Olivia made the mistake of saying, "Pardon me?"

"I'm sure you know the story," Angela began eagerly. "God went to visit Adam and Eve and said he wanted to see all their children. Eve hadn't finished bathing some of them, so she showed the clean ones to God and said they were all she had." She wagged her finger in our faces. "But you can't fool God. He knew she had more, so He said whoever she hid from Him had to be hidden from everyone. From that day forward, the unwashed children were invisible to human beings. The elves are descended from them."

Olivia rolled her eyes. "That's fascinating, Angela. So you're saying you saw an elf push Julia?" I could hear the skepticism in her voice.

Angela nodded. "I was looking out the window in the bus when I saw this elf come out of hiding. I got out and followed it. The elf hid behind those rocks over there—she swept her hand in the direction of some large boulders—and scampered to the hole when it thought no one was looking."

"Scampered?"

"It scampered up behind you and shoved. And then disappeared."

"I see. What was the elf wearing?"

Angela heehawed like a donkey. "You don't know much about the hidden people, do you? They all wear the same thing. Long capes and caps on their heads. And sometimes little suits."

Olivia and I exchanged glances. In Angela's confused mind, little suits could mean bathing suits. "Was this a male or female elf?" I asked.

"Elves are not gender specific."

This was getting ridiculous. "Please try to remember, Angela. An elf didn't push me in the water. It was someone from our group."

Angela pursed her lips. "I know what I saw. Don't you think I'd recognize a member of our group?"

Olivia shrugged. "At this point I don't think you would recognize your mother," she mumbled.

"Quiet," I warned her. But it was too late. Angela stalked out of the restroom.

"Sorry," my friend said. "That woman is nuts. I couldn't listen to anymore."

I couldn't blame Olivia, but I sure wished we could find out what Angela had seen. I pushed the door open and walked into the restaurant. Several people browsed through the shelves of snacks and souvenirs. I looked at rows of troll figurines, which seemed to be the most popular memento for visiting tourists. Outside, Christof stood next to the bus, talking to the driver.

I scanned our group looking for anyone dressed as an elf, but there was no one fitting that description. Renee and Ginger were short enough, but no one would ever say Renee was not gender specific. Her perfectly formed breasts were prominent even under her fleece jacket. And no one could miss Ginger's flaming red hair. Even tucked under a hat, errant strands peeked out. Nicole Boucher was too tall to be an elf. Emma, my favorite candidate, was a square, tank-shaped person. Elflike was not an appropriate adjective. I ruled out the men, so that left no one. But I was sure one of these people had pushed me into the water.

I involuntarily shivered.

CHAPTER NINE

"Do you think I should tell Christof that someone pushed me into the water? I know he thinks I lost my balance and fell. I also know he doesn't need any more problems. He'd probably sell his grandmother if it would hasten the end of this trip."

Olivia and I sat on the steps in front of the geothermal power plant and talked while the others toured the facility. Now I was completely convinced Lydia's death wasn't an accident, mostly because someone had tried to harm me. What did this person think I knew? My conversations with others in the group had been neither revealing nor profound. I knew nothing, but for some reason, someone thought I did.

Angela seemed to be losing more touch with reality, and I wondered if she should be sent home. "What if the poor soul wanders off somewhere," I said to Olivia. "Her family must know about her condition. You'd think they'd be concerned."

"How do you know she even has a family? Perhaps she's all alone in life." Olivia opened a bottle of water and took a long swallow.

"I wish we had someone else to talk to about all this. I mean, you're fine, but we know how each other thinks. We need fresh blood."

"What about Dirk? He felt your ass."

"First of all, he didn't. So I'm going to ignore that. And I'm leery of him because I don't know what scared Angela so badly. He does seem like a nice guy, though, but you never know. People have what I like to call 'public faces.' They're out-going and friendly as long as they're on the tour, but the minute it's over, they become the people they really are back home."

Olivia looked at me as if I were crazy, so I said, "I remember a trip Tony and I took to Canada. We were with a great bunch of people. One couple was particularly fun, and we did everything together—even promised to stay in touch once we returned home. But when the tour ended, and we were all in the airport waiting for our flights, they didn't even acknowledge us. The whole life-of-the-party behavior had been a façade—or the public face. So we have no idea who the real Dirk is. What if we're just seeing his public face."

Olivia leaned back and turned her face to the sun. "Maybe Angela is in some phase of dementia, maybe the whole thing with Dirk was fabricated in her mind. You might be judging him unfairly, but you're right. What do we know about anybody on this tour? Maybe he's an evil-tempered, corrupt legal shark and Angela somehow knows this."

I frowned. "How would she, though? He's from California and she's from Tulsa, Oklahoma. Pretty far away from each other."

"There are planes, you know. They fly all the time. And there's TV and all the social media. She could have seen him anywhere."

I shook my head. "I don't think that's it. She was on the bus with him for four days and didn't have a problem. And remember we all introduced ourselves that first night at the hotel. If she'd seen him somewhere before and was afraid of him, she would have reacted. No, it has to be something that happened here."

"Maybe you should be nicer to your ass-grabbing friend. He might be able to tell you what's going on."

This was actually a good idea. It never occurred to me to ask him.

I waited until we arrived at the Selfoss Hotel and finished the check-in process. Before Dirk could head to his room, I cornered him in the lobby.

"Would you like to go for a walk?"

"You mean right now?"

"I do, indeed."

He looked me over. "You don't want to maybe change your clothes first? I mean it's okay with me if you want to walk around in those tights, but you might stop traffic if people see you."

I felt the blood rush to my face. I'd forgotten I was wearing Olivia's borrowed ultra tight clothes. Dirk didn't have to worry about looking ridiculous because Christof had lent him gray slacks and a white sweater to replace his soaked clothes. He looked a bit like a Viking. And it had been a long time since anyone had said I was capable of bringing vehicles to a halt. I assumed he meant I looked fairly good, but on second thought, maybe he meant I looked ridiculous. Whatever. There was no way I was going one more step in these clothes.

"Can we meet in fifteen minutes?"

He shifted his camera bag from his right hand to his left. "That will be fine. I'll be here."

He started to say more, but I ran to the bus, grabbed my duffle bag just as Christof was unloading it and ran to our room. It took precisely seven minutes to put on jeans, a raspberry V-neck sweater and dry shoes. I was in the lobby before he arrived, which gave ne a chance to observe some of my fellow travelers.

George, Ginger, and Renee seemed deep in conversation. I'm not ashamed to say I moved closer so I could eavesdrop.

"I was thinking we could have a drink together this evening," George was saying. "I'd like to hear more about being a personal trainer. Ginger here is interested in becoming one. Aren't you, sweetheart?"

When his wife didn't answer, he said, "What say we meet at six thirty? The bar here looks pretty nice."

"I don't think so. I have to go now. Skip is waiting."

Renee's words were clipped and crisp. She obviously didn't want to be with these folks.

"Where is he waiting?" George asked. "I saw him head towards town with Christof."

Fury flashed over Renee's face. "Really? I'm pretty sure he's in the room. Anyway, no thank you. Excuse me. Please."

"Some people can't take a hint," she said as she passed me. "This trip is beginning to suck. Big time. And Skip didn't go anywhere with Christof. He really is in the room."

Up until then I hadn't noticed Emma sitting in a leather chair in the bar. Her glasses were perched on her nose, and she wrote furiously in her notebook. Curious, I walked over to her. When she saw me, she pressed the notebook to her chest and said, "You didn't attend the geothermal presentation. Fortunately, I took copious notes. I'll have them ready for you later."

Since I trusted no one on this trip, I wanted to have a look at what she was writing—just to see if she really was taking notes and not plotting the location of the next unfortunate "accident."

"Could I take a peek now?" I asked. "I'm so sorry I missed a fascinating discussion."

She seemed flustered. "No, I think not. These are not neatly transcribed. Can't you wait until tomorrow?"

"I suppose so. It's just that you do such a thorough job. Very detailed."

"I try," she said. "I think these trips are a waste of time if you don't absorb what you see."

I nodded. "So true. This is my first trip with Lark Tours, so I'm still getting used to traveling in a bus and having a roommate. Have you been on many, or is this your first trip, too?"

"Oh, my goodness, no. This is our thirteenth Lark tour." She lowered her voice. "Did you know when you've done several trips with them, they send you a gift when you arrive in each country? I can't wait to see what they come up with this time."

I smiled. "That sounds very nice. You must love this tour company if you have traveled with them so much."

"They offer good value," she said.

A thought occurred to me. "Have you ever been on a trip with anyone from a previous tour? I'd think that might happen with some of you veteran travelers."

She slapped her notebook into her bag and stood up. "I'm sure it might. I'll have the notes ready for you tomorrow."

I watched her hurry out and wondered what I'd said to make her exit so quickly. I pushed it out of my mind when I saw Dirk enter the lobby.

He smiled when he saw me. "I liked you in those tights. Too bad you couldn't keep them on. I'm glad, though, you want to talk," he said once we were outside. We walked along the banks of the Ölfus River under a vast gray sky. A fairly brisk wind whipped the current and made travel difficult for a small boat. "I've felt a distinct chill in the air since our day on the rock," he said, "and I wondered what I'd done."

I sighed. I still didn't know if I trusted him, but I had to talk to someone other than Olivia. And so what if I didn't trust him? In a few days this trip would be over, and we'd all be back in our respective homes. It really wasn't my job to worry about Lydia's death. But I did want to get back home on my own two feet—not the way Mrs. Cumberland would be returning—and to do that I had to make sure we stayed safe.

So I took a deep breath and said, "I was wondering why Angela was so afraid of you. I'm sure you noticed she was terrified."

"I did. At first I thought it was a reaction to being left on the rock. Then I thought maybe she was having some kind of hallucination. She does seem to go in and out of reality. I honestly have no idea why she's so afraid—other then perhaps I resemble some imaginary elf or hidden person."

It was hard to imagine Dirk as an elf. First of all, his ears didn't stick out. And he was tall. Over six feet. And muscular. Not muscle bound like Skip, but solidly built.

"So you don't know anything about her and have never had any contact with her."

He stopped walking and looked at me. "I promise you I have never seen Angela before. Or any of these people. The only one I've heard of is Dr. Boucher. A few years ago he was involved in a malpractice lawsuit. He was sued because one of his patients died, and the family accused him of negligence. I think I read he quit practicing medicine after that."

"Which might explain why he and his wife keep to themselves. Would you happen to know if Nicole was a nurse?"

"Don't know. But lots of doctors marry their nurses. It wouldn't surprise me. Why do you ask?"

I told him about going to Angela's room and finding Nicole there. "She said she'd taken Angela's pulse to make sure she was okay. That's something someone in the medical profession would do. And," I continued, "Emma Sperling told me she'd taken thirteen trips with Lark Tours. That made me think maybe Angela had also taken several trips and had traveled with one of these folks before. Like you."

"I assure you, I've never been on one of these things in my life."

I glanced at him out of the corner of my eye. "This isn't that bad, is it?"

"Well," he said, taking my hand and smiling at me, "it is beginning to have its advantages."

I didn't know why my heart started to beat faster. It must have been because we were walking up a slight incline. We passed the public swimming pool and stopped to watch people diving off the high board. It was twilight but the pool was still crowded in spite of the chilly air. These were hardy people! When we reached a small bar and restaurant, Dirk suggested a drink.

"Let's keep walking, "I said. "We can have one later if you want to." I was mentally reviewing my hair, makeup and clothes. After my involuntary plunge into the hole, my face and hair needed more than the few swipes I'd given them in the room—especially if I was going to sit across the table from someone.

Ahead of us I thought I saw Angela. She was too far away to be certain, but the figure was wearing a long skirt with a ruana around her shoulders. She walked alongside a much smaller person dressed in black pants and a gray jacket whose head was covered with a hood.

"Come on," I said to Dirk. "I'll bet that's her 'elf.' We can settle this once and for all."

I fully intended to meet this person, so I broke into a trot. Briefly. It was hard to move quickly when the hand I was holding belonged to a body that refused to move.

"I'm not going to gallop down the street," Dirk said firmly. "You're going to have to slow down."

It was too late, anyway. Angela and her little friend had disappeared.

By tacit agreement, we retraced our steps to the hotel. The lobby was crowded with folks waiting for the bar to open. As I started to my room, Dirk said, "How about a drink after dinner?" I must have looked doubtful because he said, "If you say yes, I'll tell you more about myself. Isn't that tempting for such an amateur sleuth?"

Actually, it was. What harm could one drink do?

CHAPTER TEN

We were late getting to the dining room because Olivia took forever to dry her hair. The only available seats were at a table with the Sperlings, Cameron and Angela.

"I'd almost rather skip dinner," Olivia whispered in my ear. "This is going to be dreadful."

I agreed, but there wasn't much we could do about it. Turning and leaving was out of the question. I greeted everyone pleasantly as I slid onto a chair next to Cameron. The poor man looked so pale and tired, I felt sorry for him. When he excused himself halfway through dinner, I wasn't surprised.

At least the food was delicious. I devoured the succulent langostino, which is what Icelanders call lobster. Angela apparently didn't share my enthusiasm. She sat with her arms crossed over her chest and glared at the tasty shellfish.

"You should try them, Angela," I told her. "They're delicious."

"I don't eat what I don't recognize."

I would have asked if I could have her portion, but I was afraid she might have sprinkled voodoo powder on them. "So...," I said, trying to think up something to say, "have you all traveled with Lark Tours before?"

Emma fiddled with a scarf around her neck. "I told you before. We've visited many places."

"I imagine you've met a lot of fascinating people."

"Of course," she said. "What's your point?"

"No point. I'm just making pleasant conversation. How about you, Angela? Have you taken many tours?"

She had shoved the langostino off her plate and replaced them with hunks of bread, which she smeared with butter. "I have traveled extensively," she said. "And met many people."

"I think your fellow passengers can make or break a trip," Olivia offered. "One bad apple can ruin everything."

"I concur," Emma murmured. "We certainly had an unpleasant one on this trip."

Nathan put his hand on his wife's arm. "You shouldn't say anything. I don't want you to get upset."

The color mounted in Emma's cheeks. "I'm sure you know I'm talking about Mrs. Cumberland. She was a hateful person."

"I wouldn't go that far," I said. "She wasn't a particularly warm woman but hateful seems extreme."

"You don't know anything." Emma pushed back her chair and stood up. "I have to get my medicine. I feel a migraine coming on."

We watched in silence as Emma stalked through the dining room and into the lobby. "Really, I'm sorry, Nathan," I began. "I certainly wasn't trying to upset her. I know we're all shaken up by Lydia's death."

He looked down at the napkin he was twisting in his hand. "It's okay. That's not what has her upset."

I held my breath, waiting for him to say more.

"Emma is right, you know. She really was a hateful person. I don't know how her husband could stand her."

"I understand how you could feel that way," Olivia said. "Her personality was a bit abrasive."

"It was more than that." He stopped twisting the napkin and looked at me. "Emma means everything to me. She's…well, she's pretty fragile."

Fragile? The woman could probably bench press me.

"So I'm not going to allow anyone to harm her."

"Of course not. She's a lovely woman." Lordy! The words rolled right off my tongue as if I meant them.

His body suddenly became rigid. "Then you can understand how angry it made me when Mrs. Cumberland accused my wife of stealing from her."

Whoa! What was going on here?

I hoped I looked appropriately shocked. "That's a terrible accusation. Where would she ever get such an idea?"

"As if my Emma would take anything that didn't belong to her! She was simply borrowing a medication she saw in Mrs. Cumberland's bag."

I nodded. "Of course. I see. What kind of medication would that be?"

"Something for her nerves. She's very sensitive to her surroundings, and she kept saying there was such a bad aura on the bus. Sometimes she has trouble catching her breath. She happened to see a bottle of Xanax in the bag Mrs. Cumberland left on the bus when we stopped for a bathroom break. Emma borrowed the bottle—fully intending, mind you, to return it. But Lydia suddenly appeared and saw Emma with the bottle in her hand. She called my wife a thief and threatened to tell Christof to call the authorities. It took me forever to convince her not to do that." He looked embarrassed. "I have to say, I wasn't unhappy when she died. And neither was Emma."

By nine o'clock, most folks had drifted off to bed. Dirk and I sat at a table in the bar and looked out the window at the lights sparkling on the river. There was only one other person in the room—a tourist from Norway, who sat by himself drinking aquavit.

I had consumed two glasses of wine at dinner, which was one over what I could handle well, so I certainly didn't need the one Dirk ordered for me. But I was feeling mellow and content, and it felt good to have someone else listen to all my neurotic theories.

As I talked, I gave Dirk the once-over. He looked pretty good. Blue polo shirt, khaki pants. I already mentioned his okay physique. Once again, I wondered why he was unattached. And I'd had just enough wine to ask him.

His blue eyes that had been laughing a few minutes ago became sad.

"My wife died four years ago. Of cancer. It took her so fast, we hardly knew what was happening."

Me and my big mouth! I put my hand over his and said, "I'm so sorry. I certainly didn't mean to pry. For some reason I figured you had a long list of divorces behind you."

His eyes lost some of their melancholy. "Why would you think that?"

"Because you're, well, sort of good-looking, and I can't imagine women not chasing after you." I was drowning in deep water, so I finally gave up. "You look like a guy with a lot of women."

I buried my face in my glass so he couldn't see me.

"I could say the same about you. Don't you have a long list of heartbroken lovers?"

I looked around to see who he was talking to, but his sexy eyes were staring straight at me.

"That makes me laugh. I don't have men chasing me. I can't even remember what that's like." I did, however, sit up a bit taller and suck in my stomach.

"You're very pretty. And I love your energy, even if you are a bit whacky."

"I'll bet you say that to all the girls," I simpered.

He suddenly became serious. "There aren't 'all the girls.' I have two kids. Two boys—twenty-seven and twenty-nine. They're both married. At least they used to be. Toby is divorced. He has one daughter. Jason has twin girls. We all live within two miles of each other. My family and my work are my life. I came on this trip because I discovered I'd been spending fourteen hours a day trying to defend people who had, for the most part, committed terrible crimes. I needed to recharge my batteries." He paused. "And you? Why are you here?"

"I got tired of making cupcakes."

He laughed and signaled the bartender for more wine. "That can't be all there is to your life. You're way too vibrant to settle for baking."

So I told him about my life with Tony and how I used to be a writer for the local newspaper until Tony was killed and I lost my mojo, and how Olivia, my oldest friend, and I decided to start our own business.

"And by the way, I really am a good cook and baker."

He was sensitive enough not to ask personal questions about Tony's death. For a bit we sat in companionable silence, perhaps each of us thinking about our deceased spouses.

"I grew up in the South," he said. "My father was a Yankee who couldn't stand living in the cold north. He quit his job as an account manager of a ball-bearing company and moved us to Bluffton, South Carolina. We had a little cedar-sided house on the May River. If I close my eyes I can still smell the water. It was a great place to live as a kid."

Good grief! This was amazing. "You're not going to believe this," I told him. "I was born in Beaufort! My father owned a fishing boat and took tourists out in the ocean to fish for shark and other stuff. My parents divorced when I was six and my mother took my brother and me back to her home in Iowa, which explains my lack of a southern accent. We spent many summers on the beach in Sea Pines, so I've been to

Bluffton. Have you ever eaten at the Squat and Gobble?"

"No way! You've heard of that place? My wife used to be appalled every time I suggested eating there."

I nodded. "It was one of my husband's favorite places to go when we visited Hilton Head. He couldn't wait to eat that greasy food. Might as well just shoot cholesterol directly into your veins."

We both laughed. I was feeling good. It was as if I'd known Dirk all my life. When he ordered another round of drinks, I settled back in my chair, thoroughly enjoying the conversation. And, I had to admit, also the man. He was so easy to talk to.

"So how did you end up in California?" I asked.

He looked embarrassed. "Somehow I managed to get into Stanford. Then law school. After I got my degree, I was hired by a law firm in San Francisco. I met my wife there. She was from Carmel and loved the west coast, so we never left. How about you? Have you lived in North Carolina long?"

I nodded. "I went to UNC-Chapel Hill to study journalism and met Tony in a bar. He was a student studying business at the time. Later he decided to go into law enforcement."

I should have used my head and gone to bed when the bartender said he was closing up because by now I had to squint to make my eyes focus, and my voice sounded fuzzy, even to me. But Dirk suggested going for a walk, and that seemed like a good idea. I wasn't dressed for the cool night air, so of course I snuggled against him. We walked for a bit enjoying the night and the sound of the rushing current on the river. When he said, "I have some wine in my room," it seemed completely natural to go with him.

I was in a happy, wine-induced fog outside his door, but once inside I was suddenly sober and totally aware of Dirk standing next to me. He smelled good—like soap and fresh air, and his body was solid. Oh, boy, was it solid!

"I think you know there's something good happening between us," he said huskily. "I knew you were special from the minute I met you."

I felt my knees go weak. I was fifty-four years old, I had my gray roots touched up regularly, and relied heavily on body-shaping undergarments. And I hadn't had sex in two years. Never in my wildest dreams—back in North Carolina when I was icing cupcakes—did I imagine I would be standing in a handsome man's hotel room in Iceland. And that handsome man very definitely had sex on his mind.

He pulled me to him, took my face in his hands and kissed me. My legs threatened to buckle, and I had to sternly tell myself to straighten up. Thoughts of 'he only wants me for the sex' flitted through my mind, but I chased them away.

"I'm sorry," he said as he let me go. "You just look so damn tempting."

"Why are you sorry? Do it again."

Excuse me? Did I say that? Since he was a total gentleman, he obliged. I can only say it had been a very long time since anyone had kissed me, and now I felt all kinds of forgotten sensations. Dirk ran his hand down my body, and I shivered in delight.

"Are you sure about this?" he whispered in my ear.

"Positive. Stop talking."

Later, after we kissed goodnight and I walked down the hall to my room, I felt pretty good. For the first time in my life, I'd had a one-night stand.

Olivia came running down the hall waving her arms like a windmill. I grabbed one that was flailing dangerously close to my face and said, "What's up?

You look kind of scattered." I said this because my normally elegantly clad friend was wearing striped pajama bottoms and a blue windbreaker.

"You just won't believe this," she panted. "I was on my way to the bathroom—seriously, there was something wrong with the hot dog I ate today. My stomach is on fire." She stopped talking and looked me up and down. "Where have you been? You look all funny. Kind of mushy happy, and your hair's a mess."

Before she delved deeper into my appearance, I intervened. "You were on your way to the bathroom, and..."

She ran her fingers through her hair. "I'm getting to that. When I was on my way to the bathroom, I saw a note had been slipped under the door. Take a look at this." She thrust a piece of paper in my hand. "Someone on this trip is really sick."

It looked like it was written in lipstick. Olivia peered over my shoulder as I read. "All we have to do is figure out who uses this shade. I'd say it's a sort of a dark melon. What do you think?"

I was more concerned with the message than the implement used to write it.

I saw you snooping. Leave it alone or you may not get home.

My first instinct was to turn around, knock on Dirk's door and show it to him. Right about now he was probably crawling under the covers, so he'd be all warm and....

Olivia gave me an arched eyebrow look. "What on earth is the matter with you? You have the goofiest expression on your face. I told you not to have that second glass of wine. So what do you make of the note?"

"I don't know, but on second thought, I don't think it's written in lipstick. That looks more like crayon.

And who on this trip has a large supply of pencils, pens and other colorful writing supplies?"
    We both said it in unison.
    "Emma Sperling."

CHAPTER ELEVEN

"Okay, folks. Eight of you have signed up for our exciting river rafting trip. The people not going can stay in the bus. We will park on a cliff and you can watch your friends navigate the rapids."

At Drumbó Rafting Basecamp, Renee and Skip, Ginger and George, Dirk, Cameron, Olivia and I were outfitted in wet suits, fleece jackets, life vests, some kind of rubber footies and helmets. So far I hadn't had a chance to say more than a quick "good morning" to Dirk. I'd tried to study his eyes for a hidden message, such as *Last night was unforgettable. You have the most amazing body,* but he seemed breezy and indifferent and made no mention of our recent dalliance. I told myself to forget it. We were on vacation in Iceland. This was sex without emotional attachment. It was what we one-night stand gals did.

Back in Wake Forest when I signed up for this rafting adventure, it sounded like a good idea. Now…not so much. I was surprised to see Cameron on the trip. Up until today, he'd kept to himself, which was totally understandable. I figured now he needed a bit of exercise and excitement.

The eight of us boarded a special bus for the ride to the river. As we jolted along a deeply rutted road full of stones and other obstacles, I sat in the back and tried to think up a way out. I'd had enough water fun for one trip. But I'd paid $70 for the privilege of being terrified, and I didn't intend to lose my money.

By the time we reached the banks of the Hvitá River, I'd worked myself into a swivet of uncertainty. I decided I hated water, and now I was beginning to hate myself for being so—let's call it available—last night. Or maybe a bit over-served with wine.

The river looked dangerous. Dark, pointed rocks jutted out indiscriminately, making the arctic water look like an obstacle course. And I could hear the rapids roaring in the distance. Olivia sidled over to me and said, "I think I left something on the stove. I have to go back now." I agreed with her, but we were both out of luck. We watched the bus bounce up the gravel road and disappear from sight.

Our rafting guide, Jinx, a tall, dark-haired girl in her twenties, explained the rules. "Sit on the edge of the raft. When I tell you to paddle, you must paddle. When I say lean right, what do you do? Exactly. Lean right. Or left. It is not difficult. If you fall out, do not try to stand up. You must lie on your back and point your feet forward. You will then come to us. Try not to hit the rocks. And do not try to stand up. If you do that, you will be in trouble because we cannot come back up the rapids to get you."

This did not sound like fun. If I fell out, I would automatically panic and try to stand up. And that would be that. I considered taking off my wedding ring, which I still wore, and giving it to Olivia. Just in case.

"So now please everyone take hold of the raft and carry it into the river."

It was heavy. The little rubber footies offered no protection against the stones we had to walk over. I must have put them on incorrectly because water flooded into them as soon as I stepped into the river. I was already miserable and we hadn't even started.

"We are ready," Jinx said. "How about you and you take seats in the front?" She pointed to Dirk and

Cameron. "The rest of you can sit behind them. I will be in the back steering, but it is up to you to help me guide the raft. And please do not worry. This will be fun."

Sitting on the edge of the raft didn't seem like the most stable position for survival. I perched in front of Jinx, figuring if I started to go over, maybe she would be able to grab me. I curled my fingers around the rope running around the edge of the raft and vowed not to let go—no matter what. Ginger was behind Cameron and George was behind Dirk. Skip and Renee were in front of Olivia and me.

At first, it wasn't bad—or even scary. A few gentle waves, and we paddled when Jinx yelled. But soon the raft was pitching up and down and water rushed over us. I clung to the rope for dear life and prayed I'd stay put. One particular slam of the water sent me bouncing so high, I was sure there was a foot of air between my ass and the hard rubber of the raft. This was definitely not fun. The brochure said this was a "seven kilometer adventure of thrills and magnificent scenery." Who could look at scenery? I either had my eyes closed or full of water.

"Use your paddle," Jinx yelled. "We are approaching some turbulent water."

Swell. All I wanted to do was sit on the bottom of the raft and cover my head with my hands. Nevertheless, I did my best.

"On the next rapid, you all lean to the right," our guide yelled. We did as we were told and the raft seemed to climb up like a roller coaster and then fall frighteningly. A wall of water washed over us, threatening to send us all into the river. I was sure I was drowning.

When I heard Jinx say, "You all can relax for a bit. Those were the strongest rapids we will meet," I opened my eyes and looked around. We were all doing the same thing.

Olivia was unhappy. "This will never again be on my bucket list. You have to be crazy to like this."

Renee reached for Skip's hand. Ginger looked dazed. Dirk and Cameron laughed and hoisted their paddles. It was then I noticed George was gone.

Ginger noticed at the same time. She screamed and tried to stand up. "Stop! Where's George? Someone help!"

"Stay calm," Jinx said. "This happens often. We will get him. If he does what I instructed, he will come floating to us."

I swiveled on my rubber seat and scanned the water for George. I saw terrifying rocks and swirling rapids but no man coming toward us with his toes in the air. Jinx paddled the raft in a circle. "He will be here soon. Please do not worry."

Ginger, however, worried. "He might not have remembered what to do. He could be drowning out there!"

"No, no. He will be fine," Jinx insisted. "Keep your eyes open."

We stayed calm and smiled reassuringly at Ginger, but when minutes went by and we didn't see him, I began to feel panicked. Surely we weren't going to lose another member of our group.

"There he is!" Dirk pointed to something on the right side of the raft moving towards us. As it came closer, we saw it was George, but he didn't react when we yelled at him. Jinx kept the raft moving in a circle until he was close enough to pull in. It was hard work because George was unconscious.

Dirk and Skip stretched him out on the bottom of the raft while the rest of us paddled. Ginger fluttered her hands, trying to lift up his head. "What's wrong with him? Why isn't he talking?"

"Did he drown?" Renee looked at him with clinical interest. "Shouldn't someone do CPR?"

Dirk was already on his knees, straddling George's body. "I don't think he's swallowed much water. There's a lump on the back of his head. He may have hit it on a rock. Thank God he remembered Jinx's instructions and stayed on his back. Otherwise..." He let his words trail off, but we all knew what he left unsaid.

We cheered when George sputtered and tried to sit up. Ginger threw her arms around his neck and began to cry. "What happened to you, my poor baby? I was so worried."

"Will someone peel her off me?" George was rapidly returning to his old, pleasant self. "My head hurts like hell."

"What happened, man? We hit a rapid and you were like gone. Where's your paddle?" Skip leaned over the side of the raft looking for the elusive piece of equipment.

George sat up and felt the back of his head. "I suddenly felt like I was going to puke. And I was dizzy. Must have passed out. The food is lousy here."

The knock on his head must have knocked out his common sense because the food in Iceland was sensational. The salmon and char were unbelievably fresh, and the yogurt-like dessert called *skyr* was better than any yogurt back home. My favorite food was Icelandic lobster, or langostino. Sweet, tender meat from pristine waters. For a restaurant man, George sure didn't recognize good food, which made him an idiot in my book.

Relieved that she had no customer with a serious injury, Jinx told us to paddle hard. There was soup, bread and beer waiting at the basecamp.

CHAPTER TWELVE

The lentil soup smelled wonderful. We were all happy to be back at the Drumbó basecamp. Now that our feet were on dry land, and there was no danger of being washed away in the river, we were feeling a bit smug about our adventure.

"I don't know how you did it," Emma said. "It looked terrifying from up on the cliff."

"Nothing to it," Olivia said. This from a woman whose face was still the color of chalk.

While I chatted with those who hadn't been on the rafting trip, my eyes roamed around the room searching for Dirk. He still hadn't said much to me, even when we helped carry the raft out of the water and across the sand to the bus. Granted, we hadn't been alone, but he could have said something. Even a wink or a secret smile would have been great. But there was no sign he remembered anything about last night. He was impersonally pleasant. Now he leaned against the bar and talked to Serge.

I wandered away from Emma and strolled casually to the end of the room and looked out the picture window. I had no interest in the view. I was waiting for Dirk to see I was alone and come talk to me. I realized as I stood there this was something I'd done in high school. My heart was even beating as fast as it had back then. I waited and waited, but he didn't seem to notice me. Out of the corner of my eye, I saw him clap Serge on the shoulder and move to the bar. He must have said something funny because the girl behind the counter laughed.

I tried to convince myself it didn't matter, but it did. I'd had no practice at casual sex without commitment, but surely the lady was entitled to something the next day. At least a perfunctory, "thank you very much," or an acknowledgement that the man recognized the lady and remembered her name.

Disgusted with myself and equally disgusted at the tears threatening to spill out of my eyes, I started down the hall toward the ladies room. As I rounded the corner, I heard familiar voices. Skip was leaning casually against the wall talking to Ginger. I stopped and listened.

"Are you hitting on me?" Ginger sounded firmer than usual. Her voice was still mellifluous, but now there was a bite to it.

"I'm not hitting on you. How could I do that? I'm married. All I said was your hair always looks gorgeous. So soft and sexy. How do you keep it so perfect looking?"

"Hairspray," was the quick reply. "And please don't touch it."

"No kidding, Ginger, with a little training you could be a knockout. Too bad you don't live close to me. I could help you." I heard the familiar laugh. "It would be a pleasure."

"And you don't call that hitting on me?"

"Nope. Just being friendly. Do you want me to hit on you?"

"I don't. You'd be wasting your time. We should go find the others."

Oh oh. I had to make my presence known before they saw me lurking in the shadows. I straightened up and walked towards them. "Hi, guys. Quite a raft ride, wasn't it.?"

Ginger looked embarrassed, but Skip gave me one of those blinding smiles and put his arm around my shoulder. "Let's go get us some of that soup. I've worked up an appetite."

Dirk was still acting like I was invisible so when Olivia said she needed a beer, I joined her at the bar. More folks had the same idea, so there were at least five people between Dirk and me. I cackled so loudly at something Olivia said, she poked me in the ribs. "You're sort of behaving oddly. Like you're high on something. What's up?"

"Don't be absurd," I replied gaily. "I'm just having a fantastic time. This has been an absolutely terrific day. Best one yet."

"You're making me worried. Did something happen that I don't know about? Did you confront Emma about the note?"

Good grief! The note. I'd forgotten all about it. "No," I told my friend. "I haven't said anything to her. I have to give it a bit more thought."

"Then what's going on? You're not normal, that's for sure."

"What is normal? And why do we put so much emphasis on being normal? Maybe it would be fun to be abnormal. You know, do whatever you want and not care what people think. Like, for instance, have sex and have it mean nothing." I furiously blinked back the tears threatening to spill down my cheeks.

Olivia's eyes narrowed to slits. "What are we talking about here? I'm having a hard time following you. Is there something we might need to discuss?" Suddenly her eyes flew open. "It's about Dirk, isn't it? Were you with him last night? I thought you looked funny. Did you sleep with him? You did, didn't you! Why didn't you tell me? We could have talked about it. Did you expect him to be all romantic this morning?"

"I don't want to talk about it. And keep your voice down. Nothing happened." I picked up my mug of beer and downed half of it.

Olivia was like a dog with a bone. "Nothing happened? Will you swear to that?"

"Leave me alone," I said crossly. "There's nothing to tell. And now I'm getting annoyed."

To avoid further conversation, I picked up my beer and slid onto a bench next to Cameron at one of the trestle tables. His head was bowed over a bowl of soup, and he didn't look up when I sat down. He was obviously not interested in conversation. But I was. I needed to stop Olivia from yammering at me.

"Did you enjoy the river rafting, Cameron?"

Spoon poised in mid-air, he said, "I suppose I did."

"Me, too. Although I must admit I was a little afraid. You must have been, too, sitting there in the front."

He shrugged. "Doesn't much matter to me what happens."

"Please don't say that. I know life seems bleak right now, but it gets better. I promise you." I was about to launch into an example from my personal history, but he cut me off.

"I really don't care whether it gets better or not, but thank you for trying to cheer me up. I just wish we hadn't come on this trip."

"I can understand that, but maybe it would have happened anyway. You know…when your number's up, it's up, and all that." I paused. "Have you heard anything from the authorities in Reykjavik?"

"Only that they don't yet have the results of the autopsy." He put down his spoon and turned to face me. "What I don't get is why she wanted to come to Iceland. Lydia liked to travel to posh places and stay in posh hotels. She knew this would be, well, primitive, but she absolutely insisted she wanted to go—even though I told her we could take a cruise on the French Riviera instead. She didn't even have the right clothes for"—he waved his hand around—"all this. It simply isn't, or wasn't, her style."

"That does seem odd," I said. "Maybe she wanted to try something new."

Cameron shook his head. "She didn't like change. We always went to the same places and stayed in the same hotels. South of France, Tuscany, sometimes London and Paris to shop. Her favorite was the Four Seasons. That's what she liked to do. Eat well and shop."

I drained my beer. "Sounds like you two had a great life. Most people can't afford vacations like that."

"Lydia didn't grow up wealthy. In fact, she had a tough life. Graduated from high school and went to work as a receptionist at a pest control company. Her mother was struggling to raise three kids by herself, so Lydia pretty much had to pay her own way. She never knew her father. Her younger brother died a few years ago. She never told me the full story, but I know it devastated her."

I shook my head when the server asked if I wanted another beer. Cameron, however, accepted. "That's a rough beginning, "I said. "But life obviously got better for her."

"Not for a while. She married a bum who treated her badly. She never talked about him and would stop me every time I tried to ask questions. He apparently worked odd jobs and lived on what Lydia earned. She had to take a second job to support both of them."

He sighed a huge sigh that came from deep in his soul. "She worked evenings cleaning office buildings. One particular building was a law office. She gradually became friendly with one of the high-powered lawyers. He was quite a bit older and in a loveless marriage. One evening she went to work and was devastated to learn this man had died. But she was supremely surprised when his will was read and he'd left a huge fortune all to her. His wife immediately sued, and I guess for a while it was messy. But his will was ironclad and Lydia was able to keep all the money. She kicked the bum out and moved far away."

He colored slightly. "I'm afraid she didn't know how to act with money. She really was a warm person, but most of the time she didn't come across that way. But I loved her."

This was quite a story. He stopped talking when Renee slithered over, put her hand on his shoulder and said, "How are you doing? I hope you know Skip and I are here for you if you need anything."

I didn't know why she couldn't speak without thrusting her breasts in his face, but apparently they moved in unison with her mouth.

"I'm good, thank you," he said. "You are kind to ask. It's people like you who make me feel better."

Renee patted him on the top of his head and gave me a smug look of satisfaction. She bounced away and seconds later I saw her talking to Dirk. She stood very close to him and looked up adoringly. And being a man, he looked pleased. They made quite a pair—Renee and Skip. I wondered why they were on this trip—and why they were married.

Copious amounts of beer were making our group noisy—that and relief at still being alive after the harrowing raft ride. Emma circulated among the group distributing digital photos of the adventure.

"I'm so thrilled with my little portable printer. I made these pictures and wrote a little story about the Hvitá River."

I looked at the paper she handed me. She had drawn water and rocks and a raft with eight primitive figures in it. And it was colorful. Very colorful. Which reminded me I needed to speak her about the note.

"This is very nice. You sure have a good assortment of crayons and colored pencils. Do you ever lend them to anybody?"

She hugged a photo to her chest. "Certainly not. I need them for my work."

"I see. What else do you use them for? Besides travel notes."

Was I imagining it or did she look uncomfortable?

"Why, nothing. What are you talking about?"

"I recently saw something written in crayon and wondered if it was from you."

"I don't know. I've given copies of my notes to nearly everyone on the trip."

She was definitely squirming. "It wasn't one of your usual notes. I was just wondering if you wrote anything besides trip notes with your pencils and crayons."

"The answer is no. Now if you'll excuse me, the others want their photos."

I watched her scurry away, realizing I'd been less than subtle with my questions. Now she knew I suspected her of writing the note, which may not be a good thing.

George had fully recovered from his recent dip in the river. Beer was helping. It sloshed out of the glass he was holding as he approached Angela. He'd had just enough alcohol to make him do something stupid.

"Hey, Angela!" he yelled. "I think one of your hidden people tried to kill me today."

The chatter in the room stopped.

"The hidden people are everywhere," she intoned.

"Yeah, so you say. But one tried to do me in today. Did you send him? Or it?"

Dirk walked over to George and put his arm around his shoulder. "You don't want to scare Angela, do you?

Why don't you join me and have some of this fine soup."

George shook himself free. "Butt out. I'm talking to the witch lady here. So tell me, witch lady, where do you find them? Do you look under rocks? Or in the trunks of trees?" George leered at Angela with bloodshot eyes. His hair was a tangled mess and he had red blotches on his cheeks.

Angela didn't seem to notice. Her eyes took on a far away expression as she said, "They are everywhere."

Dirk tried again. "Come on, man. Have something to eat." This time he grabbed George's arm firmly. Skip sauntered over and stood on the other side of George.

"I know you did it!" he yelled as they led him away. "Someone tried to poison me and I'm betting it was one of your stupid hidden people!"

Dirk and Skip managed to get George outside, but the rest of us followed. Even though I was acutely aware of Dirk's presence next to me, at the moment I was only interested in hearing what George had to say. I tried to ignore Dirk and said, "Why do you think someone tried to poison you?"

George focused his eyes on me. "Someone *did* poison me. One minute I was fine and the next thing I knew I had a terrible burning in my gut and had to puke. I'm positive someone poisoned me. I've never been sick a day in my life. After I puked, I got dizzy. Must have fallen out of the raft."

"But who would do that, George?" I asked. "And more to the point, why?"

"I don't know, but I reckon the witch does. She's into all that voodoo stuff," he said, pointing to Angela.

"George," I said, "what did you eat this morning before we went on the rafting trip? That might give us a clue."

"The normal breakfast stuff. And some of the chocolate from the little bag of candy. I figured we all got some."

"What bag of candy? I didn't see any." I automatically swung my eyes to Dirk, then realized what I was doing and looked at Renee instead. "Did you see any?"

"Nope. But I don't eat stuff like that." She patted her flat stomach. "Candy is poison."

"Exactly," George yelled. "Someone tried to poison me."

I appealed to the others, who were now clustered around. "Did any of you see little bags of candy? Did you, Ginger?"

She shook her head. "I don't know what he's talking about."

"You're trying to make me sound crazy," he yelled at his wife. "I was coming out of my room early. I get up before she does." He jerked a thumb at Ginger. "I like to have coffee in peace before the nagging starts. Anyway, there was this little cellophane bag of candy on the floor outside the door. I reckoned everyone got one."

"Was there one for Ginger, too?" I asked.

He shook his head. "I only saw one. There was some chocolate and some gummy stuff. It tasted pretty good."

"I don't think you were poisoned," Renee volunteered. "Maybe you had a reaction to alcohol. You do drink a lot."

Dirk stepped in and said, "Why don't we let it go for now? You seem fine, George. I suggest we thank the folks for this exciting adventure and then take the bus back to the hotel. We could all use a rest."

As the others gathered up their bags and proceeded to the bus, I hung back to walk with George. "I'm glad you feel better," I said. "Stomach stuff can be nasty."

"I know I was poisoned," he said gruffly. "I felt fine last night after dinner. In fact, some of us went into town for a nightcap."

"Really? I was out, too." I hoped my face wasn't flaming as I remembered where I'd been. "Were you with some of our group?"

"Yep. Serge and Nicole. They're okay people. And of course, Ginger, and Renee and Skip. I thought I remembered Skip from years ago. I used to do bodybuilding, and I thought I recognized him from a competition. But he said no." He shrugged. "Those guys pretty much all look the same."

Ginger was waiting for us at the bus. She tucked her hand around her husband's arm and gave me what I interpreted as a dirty look. "He needs to sit down and be quiet."

"Fine with me," I said. I needed to sit down myself.

CHAPTER THIRTEEN

"So what do we have here?" I said to Olivia. She was lying on her bed with her *Nobody Home* sleep mask across her eyes, but I knew she was listening. "Angela has lost touch with reality but knows something about Lydia's death. Emma probably wrote the note we found under our door. But why? George thinks he was poisoned, and he did get sick enough to fall overboard. Where did this suspicious candy come from? And someone pushed me into the swimming hole. I am absolutely sure of that. What do you think about all this?"

Olivia ripped the mask off her face. "That isn't what I'm interested in at the moment. I want to know about you and Dirk. And don't tell me nothing happened because I know it did." Her voice softened. "It's okay, you know. We're on vacation. You're having a fling." She studied my face intently. "It didn't mean anything, though, did it? You don't care about him, do you? Because you know that would be silly. You won't see him again after this trip."

"This morning he acted like he didn't know me," I said in a small voice.

"What did you expect him to do?" She shook her head. "You should have told me you were thinking about sleeping with him. I could have given you some pointers. One-night stands are just that. One night. Good sex. No emotional ties. Dirk's a good-looking man. He's probably had a million of them."

"I don't think so. He said he hasn't."

"And you believed that? Oh, boy! I really wish you and I could have talked before you went to his room. You needed to know the rules for casual sex. There are some, you know."

"I didn't know I was going to his room!" I yelled. "It was all very spontaneous. Too much wine, no sex for years, a good-looking man in a foreign country. It was probably inevitable."

Olivia sat up and retrieved her brush from the bedside table. As she tried to tame her tangled mass of hair, she said, "I just don't want you running around here with a broken heart. Because he isn't. He knows the rules. It is what it is. You had fun. He had fun. And that's it."

I heard what she was saying, but in my heart I couldn't believe that. Surely Dirk wasn't the kind of man who could tenderly make love to a woman and then forget her the next day, because I sure wasn't that kind of a woman.

"I probably need to talk to him, though. Just for a second."

Olivia shook her head. "Let it go, sweetie. I understand the urge, but you'll only feel worse if he doesn't have time for you."

"You don't understand. I left something in his room and I need to get them back."

Olivia stopped brushing and arched her eyebrows. "What exactly did you forget?"

I felt my face turn hot. "My panties. And I don't see what's so funny that you have to reach for a tissue to wipe your eyes."

"I'm sorry," she gasped between bouts of laughter. "But only you could do that. I hope at least they are wispy pieces of black lace, although I must admit I've never seen you wear anything like that."

"They are cotton Jockeys," I mumbled. "But they are French cut."

A knock on the door interrupted her merriment. When I opened it, Angela stood there.

"Come with me now. We can talk to the hidden people."

She seemed perfectly normal but that didn't mean her mind wasn't spinning like a hamster on a wheel. Christof had told me in strictest confidence the tour company had tried—with no luck—to contact her family. I wasn't crazy about the idea of going out with her alone so I said, "It's getting kind of late, Angela. Are you sure you want to do this tonight?"

"I thought you wanted to see them. They're quite agitated after today's activities"

"What activities do you mean?" I asked. Maybe she wasn't as okay as she seemed.

"The problem with the potion."

Oh boy! I had to hear this. I told Olivia I'd be right back and shut the door. "You mentioned a potion," I said as I ran down the hall to keep up with her long strides. "Does someone have a potion?"

"Yes. It didn't work right. It was supposed to make him invisible, but it didn't. Gudrun said he would be invisible in the water and no one would ever be able to see him again. He would become a *huldufólk*. It was really going to be quite exciting, you know. He would be among us but no one would know that. But something went wrong. Gudrun said he wasn't supposed to get back in the boat."

This statement made my stomach lurch. Was she talking about George? It sounded like invisible meant dead. We reached the lobby where I saw Dirk using one of three computers available for guests. He looked up as we rushed past him, and I had time to see him raise his eyebrows questioningly. Good. He was still able to recognize me.

Once outside, Angela raced down the steps and headed toward the hills behind the hotel. I wasn't crazy about following her. It would have been one thing to walk toward town where there were still lights and people, but the hills were dark, and I had no idea what Angela was up to. And this Gudrun—whoever she was—didn't sound like a nice person. Still, this might be my only opportunity to see the elusive "elf" that was talking to Angela. I had to go with her. And it was not reassuring when she pulled out a pocket flashlight that cast a weak beam on the ground.

We had walked about fifty feet when Angela held out her hand like a traffic cop. "We have to be quiet now. The hidden people live up here. At least Gudrun does. I'm not sure about the others."

"Who is Gudrun? Are we meeting her? Does she live in a house?" I asked hopefully. Because there wasn't one in sight. All I could make out in the darkness was the outline of trees.

"No house. They don't live in houses. They live in trees and rocks and such. She said she'd be here tonight. I think she wants to meet you"

I stopped in my tracks. "Have you actually seen this Gudrun? Why do you think she wants to meet me."

"Of course, I've seen her. What kind of a question is that? I couldn't take you to her if I'd never seen her, now could I? I met her a long time ago when she looked like someone else. And I think she wants to meet you because she's always asking me about you—like what do you and Olivia talk about and things like that."

"Does she now?" This was interesting. "What do you mean 'when she looked like someone else'? Have you perhaps confused her with somebody?"

"No. I said, 'I know you' and she said, 'I am a hidden person now. No one else can see me unless I want them to.'"

I tried not to show Angela how alarmed I felt. She had lost so much touch with reality, she was now making no sense. I wished I had Olivia or Dirk with me.

"You said hidden people don't like to be seen. Maybe she'll hide from us."

"Are you going to keep giving me trouble, Julia? Because if so, we can go back. You don't believe in trolls and elves anyway."

"Oh, but I do. You've convinced me."

I heard her snort in the darkness. "You have to stop talking now. We're getting very close."

In spite of absolutely not believing in elves, trolls or hidden people, I felt my heart beat faster. Unless Angela was totally demented—which was still a possibility—we were going to meet someone who most likely did not live in a tree. And when Angela began to speak in tongues, I was sure I should make a run for the hotel.

"*Lítill álfur, lítill álfur!*"

"Stop it, Angela! What are you doing?" I resisted the urge to put my hand over her mouth.

"It means 'little elf.' Gudrun taught me how to say it. It's the way I call her. Then she knows it's me and not someone trying to trick her out of hiding. She will be so happy to see me because I have some things for her."

Good grief! "What kind of things?"

"Things she asked for—paper from Dirk's wastebasket, Nicole's address book. I also found some cigarettes and this little book, but it's in funny writing." She aimed the thin beam of light on the cover of a book—*Mýrin* by Arnaldur Indridason. Someone on our trip was reading a book *in* Icelandic?

"Where did you find this?" I asked. "Are you sure it belongs to someone in our group?"

"Positive. It was on the bus. I also have Olivia's wallet. I couldn't find anything of yours."

I snatched the wallet out of her hand. "You can't take things like that. Olivia looked all over for it this morning. What on earth is the matter with you?"

Not the smartest thing I've ever said, but come on, she was stealing stuff.

Her chilly voice said, "You have to leave now. You can't meet Gudrun. She wouldn't like you."

"I'm sorry, Angela," I said. "I didn't mean to make you mad, but you can't go around taking people's possessions. Maybe paper from a wastebasket is okay, but certainly not a wallet."

She sniffed. "Go away."

"Come on," I said, jovially taking her arm. "Let's keep going. We've come this far."

She shook her head. Out of the corner of my eye, I saw a dark figure emerge from the trees and silently slip away. The figure was small enough to be an elf. I pointed to the retreating shape. "Could that be Gudrun? Maybe we can run and catch up with her." I was pretty sure we were dealing with a real flesh-and-blood person and not an invisible elf.

"No," she insisted. "We have to go back. She doesn't want to see you. I can tell she's angry."

I couldn't chitchat any longer. The figure was getting away. I grabbed the flashlight out of Angela's hand and started to run.

"Hey! You can't do that!" She sounded upset, but I didn't hear feet thundering behind me. Hopefully, she'd turn around and follow the lights back to the hotel.

I had no idea where I was going, but I had to try to see the elusive Gudrun. The beam from the flashlight was so dim, I concentrated on watching my feet to avoid tripping—which is the reason I didn't see a hand reach out and grab me until it was too late. I yelled, "Let go!" but I was so startled, I stumbled along for a short distance without trying to break free. The person holding me and I veered off the path and into the woods and suddenly the flashlight fell out of my hands and it was totally dark.

"Stop snooping."

The voice was low and menacing. I couldn't tell if it belonged to a man or a woman. I was so scared I said the first thing that came into my mind. "Are you an elf?"

The person laughed. "What do you think?"

I couldn't answer because whoever it was put a cloth over my nose and my knees suddenly buckled. As I sank to the ground, I felt other hands roughly pull me to my feet.

"Stand up. And take deep breaths. Do you hear me?"

Barely. I took ragged gulps of air into my lungs and tried to steady myself. When I could stand without falling over, I looked at the person standing next to me. It was Dirk.

"It's a good thing I saw you leave with Angela," he said. "I followed you because, quite frankly, she scares me."

"Where did she go?" I asked weakly. "We were going to meet one of her hidden people. Except it's not an elf or anything like that. The hand that grabbed me was a real hand." I leaned against his strong body, which felt really good until I remembered I was mad at him for ignoring me.

"Angela took off running when she saw me," he said. "I'm sure she's back at the hotel. So let's go. We need to be back there, too."

I let him lead me out of the woods and onto the path. His flashlight was a no-nonsense, heavy-duty thing that illuminated our way quite nicely. Dirk seemed annoyed. I had to scramble to keep up with him, which wasn't easy in my wobbly state.

"Why do I have such a bad smell in my nose? Something is making me feel sick."

"Whoever grabbed you put a chloroform soaked rag over your face. This person clearly had something unpleasant in mind for you."

I shuddered. This was too much. All I wanted to do was go back to North Carolina and bake quiches.

"Hurry up," Dirk said briskly. "Since I don't know what's going on, I want to get you safely back in the hotel."

I stopped walking. "Why are you being so cold?" I yelled at his retreating back. "I'm scared to death, and you're acting terrible."

"I'm sorry you think I'm acting terrible," I heard him say. "I'm trying to keep you safe."

"Why didn't you talk to me this morning? I mean, you could have at least acknowledged you knew me after last night." I felt my face flame, but he couldn't see it in the dark. With my dignity in shreds, I ran to catch up with him. There was no way I was staying out there by myself.

"Maybe you shouldn't worry about me talking and worry more about whoever is trying to hurt you," he said. "This is a serious situation, Julia, and I don't think you're taking it seriously enough."

Actually, I was terrified. My knees were still banging together like castanets, but I didn't want to tell him that. He didn't seem in a mood to comfort me.

"I'm plenty worried," I said defensively. "We never should have continued with this trip. If the babbling Angela is right, someone among us killed Lydia. And Angela is positively nuts. She should be sent home before she causes someone or herself real harm."

"I agree with you. But I also think she knows something about Lydia's death. And we have to face the fact that someone was waiting for her—and you—to come out here tonight. I don't know who could be feeding this hidden folk nonsense to Angela, but I think we need to find out."

I stalked ahead of him. "Don't talk to me anymore. I absolutely cannot understand you." I pushed the door to the hotel open and walked into the lobby. He was being a first-class jerk.

CHAPTER FOURTEEN

Originally we were scheduled to return to Reykjavik for one night and then continue on to the north, but Christof decided to circumvent that city and proceed directly to Akureyri, which meant a very long bus ride. Olivia and I settled into our usual seats in the back. Today Renee and Skip, who normally preferred to sit behind the driver, were directly in front of us. Olivia opened her cavernous tote bag and pulled out two rolls filled with smoked salmon and slices of onion.

"These tasted so good at breakfast, I thought we should have more." She handed one to me. "Make sure you eat all of it. Onion breath should keep you out of trouble."

"Very funny." I pointed to the seat in front of us. "Let's not chat right now."

"Where is he, by the way?" Olivia can sometimes be absolutely obtuse.

"I have no idea. And please zip it."

I did know where Dirk was, though. He was sitting by himself three seats ahead of us, across from Emma and her husband. I needed to forget about him so I concentrated on eating my roll. I couldn't help thinking though. A week ago we were fourteen strangers and now we were thrown together in a situation no one could have predicted. Dirk was convinced one of us had killed Lydia. And someone was certainly trying to scare me. I still couldn't believe anyone intended me real harm, although the plunge into the underground grotto came close. As my eyes roamed around the bus, I wondered what secrets we were all harboring. And who among us was capable of murder.

Renee seemed annoyed with Skip. When he tried to talk to her, she put on her headphones and closed her eyes. Angela sat by herself and was uncharacteristically quiet. She stared out the window and ignored anyone's attempt at conversation. Was she really as batty as she seemed, or was it all an act? She seemed to be losing touch with reality more and more each day, but she'd managed to find her way to Iceland by herself, and that meant dealing with a passport and tickets and a travel itinerary. The Bouchers both slept with eyeshades firmly in place. Emma scribbled in a notebook while her husband read. Cameron sat with his arm across his forehead, obviously not in the mood to talk and George and Ginger Reilly sat with their heads bowed. I couldn't tell if they were sleeping, reading or praying.

After about two hours into the trip, Christof announced we would be making a rest stop. "You can also buy nice woolen things here. Or some trolls, if someone wishes. Not live ones," he added hastily. "Nice little statues."

Olivia applied lipstick and ran a comb through her hair. "Finally! Some shopping! I can't tell you how much I need to spend some money."

As the bus pulled off the road, I wondered what she would find to buy at this place. It was a typical Icelandic small wooden structure and didn't look like it held the high quality stuff Olivia liked to buy.

It was stuffy inside the shop. The shelves were piled high with woolen hats, gloves and scarves, and the aisles were so narrow it made me itch to walk through them. One side of the shop was devoted to evil-looking trolls.

Most of our group left quickly. I lingered because Olivia thought she wanted to buy a sweater. While she discussed the price with the shop owner, I walked down an aisle to look at cute handmade potholders fashioned in the likeness of elves and trolls. As I debated buying some for future gifts, I heard voices from somewhere behind me. One I immediately recognized as Angela's. The other sounded sort of familiar but spoke with an accent.

"I did everything you asked me to," Angela said. "Why won't you give it to me?"

"You still haven't finished what you were asked to do," the voice said. "Why not?"

"I told you. She's never alone. Besides, I don't like doing things like that. It will make the hidden people mad."

"I'm one of the hidden folks and I want you to do this. We won't be angry."

I could hear Angela snort. "Technically, I don't think you're from the *huldufólk*. You didn't know the story about Gilitrutt and everyone should know that. And trolls abduct people, but you couldn't do that either. I'm beginning to think you've had your powers taken away. Maybe you've even been banished from the rock where you live."

"Don't be silly. And be careful what you say," the voice warned. "You don't want to become invisible and live in a tree, do you?"

I had to see who owned the mysterious voice. Rather than call out and startle them, I crept to the end of the aisle, ready to meet the elusive elf/troll. Unfortunately, I felt a tap on my shoulder. "You come with me now, please." It was the shop owner and she had a scowl on her face.

I put a finger to my lips and said, "Shh. Not now." But it was too late. I heard rapid footsteps and knew Angela and the other voice were gone. I turned to the woman and said, "What's the problem?"

"Your friend is trying to pay for a very expensive sweater with some kind of strange coupons. She must buy it because she has already stretched the neck."

I followed her to where Olivia was tapping her fingers on the wooden counter. She held several coupons from our shop in her hand. "This person won't take these in payment. I offered her two dozen chocolate swirl, caramel cupcakes plus a dozen assorted flavors, but she wouldn't accept them."

I studied my friend closely to see if she had suddenly suffered some crucial misfiring of brain synapses. She seemed to be okay so I said, "Why don't you let me pay for the sweater and we can chat about this later. I'm sure you realize this nice lady is probably never going to set foot in our little lunchroom in Wake Forest, North Carolina."

She pulled me aside and whispered in my ear, "Listen, this sweater is very badly made. I don't want it anymore. It isn't even worth one of our lovely cupcakes."

"That doesn't matter," I said as I pulled money out of my purse. "You stretched it so you buy it. And what is more annoying, this nonsense prevented me from learning the identity of Angela's elf. They were in the aisle behind me, and I almost was able to yell, 'Ah ha!'" As the shop owner handed me change, I asked, "How were you going to shop if you have no money? I thought you were looking forward to buying things."

"Oh, I have money," Olivia said as we pushed through the door. "I just didn't want that sweater. I think we could have gotten away with it if you hadn't been so righteous."

I should have known.

I clomped across the parking lot and scanned the area for our group. The Bouchers and Emma and Nathan were seated at a picnic table drinking bottles of lemonade. I spotted Dirk and Cameron standing behind the bus. Cameron was probably smoking. I didn't know what his habits had been before, but since Lydia's death he smoked every time the bus stopped. His clothes reeked of cigarettes, but who were we to deny the poor man some kind of comfort. Renee and Ginger walked together, deep in conversation. At one point, Renee patted Ginger's shoulder. Skip strolled out of the men's room just as Christof announced it was time to board the bus.

I looked around for George. When he banged the men's room door open and hurried to his wife, I sighed with relief. But where was Angela?

"Not again," Christof muttered. "That woman is a problem."

I certainly agreed with him. Where in the world was that woman? Since I knew she hadn't been alone in the shop, I was worried the unknown person had somehow harmed our batty traveler. Much as I hated to do it, I waited to approach Dirk until he was alone. Quickly I told him about my overheard conversation in the shop.

"She was definitely talking to someone with an accent and it sounded like a woman's voice, but it could have been a man. I'm kind of worried about her now."

Dirk's face creased in concern. "You have no idea who it could be?" he asked as his eyes searched the landscape. "Two of the men have what I would call tenor voices—Boucher and Cameron. Could it be one of them?"

"I don't know. This person threatened to make Angela invisible and make her live in a tree."

Dirk smiled down at me. "Really? Do you think we should go check out the foliage around here?"

Embarrassed, I turned to leave. "That's exactly what I'm going to do. You can laugh all you want, but there was something menacing about the voice. I think Angela is in trouble."

He easily kept up with me as I stalked away. "I'm certainly not going to let you wander around by yourself. You tend to get into trouble when you're alone."

"I can't imagine you would care." I sounded like a petulant teenager, but since Dirk was the only man I had, ah, ever known in the biblical sense since my husband, I felt I had the right to expect some sort of comment after the event.

"Actually," he said, "I do care."

"It doesn't really matter to me whether you do or not." Boy, was that a lie. Casual sex just wasn't working for me. I didn't expect a lifelong commitment, but I expected something. Even a brief "nicely done," would have sufficed. But before I could hear anymore, we saw Angela.

And she was in a tree.

She sat on a gnarled branch of a pine tree about ten feet off the ground. And she looked terrified.

"Angela!" I called. "Can you get down from there?"

"You can't see me. Go away."

"I'm pretty sure we can. Come on. The bus is leaving."

"Gudrun made me invisible and told me I had to live up here forever."

"Gudrun is wrong. I can see you and you need to get down. How in the world did you get up there?"

"Gudrun did a spell and then I was here. She said no one would ever notice."

"Again, wrong. I'm coming up to get you."

Dirk grabbed me by the back of my shirt. "Don't think so, cupcake. That's not very smart. Look."

Angela was trying to stand up on the branch.

"Don't do that!" I screamed. "Are you crazy?"

"Not the best choice of words," Dirk said as he pushed past me. "Angela, listen to me. Sit down on the branch and when I say, 'Go,' let yourself fall."

"Now who's crazy?" I yelled. "She can't do that."

Dirk eyed me calmly. "Certainly she can. I'll catch her."

"First of all, she's afraid of you. Remember? And secondly, and I'm not doubting your masculine qualities here, but she'll squash you like a bug. Angela has significant poundage."

But Dirk wasn't listening. He was texting on his phone. Within minutes, Christof arrived with Skip. "Now the poundage you're worried about will be distributed," he said. "The interesting question is—who put her up there, because she sure as hell isn't doing these stupid things all by herself."

If Angela was afraid of Dirk, she didn't show it. She seemed almost in a trance as she sat down on the branch. She closed her eyes and stuck out her arms. Christof took over issuing the orders.

"Do not do that, Angela. Open your eyes. And put your arms down. You don't want to fall on them." When she was finally in the correct position, he said, "Now just slip down. We'll catch you."

A normal person would have said, "no way," but Angela was far from normal. She slid off the branch and sailed into the waiting arms of the strong men. All three plus Angela splatted onto the ground in a tangle of arms and legs.

By now the rest of the group had joined us. "What are we doing?" Renee asked. "Is it some kind of game?"

Skip pulled Angela's heavy woolen skirt off his face and yelled, "A little help here! I think my hand is broken. Get off me, Angela! Man, you must weigh a ton."

Angela seemed unable to get to her feet. She rolled back and forth over the groaning men until helpful hands hauled her upright. As Dirk and Skip slowly stood up, the Bouchers moved among them looking for injuries.

"Your hand isn't broken," Nicole told Skip. "It's just bruised. "I'm more concerned about Dirk's face. It looks like he caught an elbow in his eye."

Indeed, it was red and swelling rapidly. Otherwise, everyone seemed to be okay.

"There's no use asking how she got there," Christof said as we all walked to the bus. "I am sure she does not know herself. This is getting to be quite a problem. We still have not been able to reach her emergency contact person." He shook his head. "She should not be on this trip. And she should not be alone." He stopped walking and looked at me. "Perhaps if you and your friend could…well, keep an eye on her? You ladies are not traveling with husbands, and I thought perhaps…"

I interrupted before he could finish. "Are you suggesting she share rooms with us? Because if you are, I don't think that will work." I didn't add for that to work I'd have to as batty as Angela. "And I'm sure Olivia wouldn't agree to it either."

"No, no," he said hastily. "I mean perhaps walk with her when we have excursions and watch when she talks to someone. I am terribly concerned something horrible is going to happen."

"Which is exactly why I don't want Julia involved." Dirk, who had been walking ahead, turned around to face us. "Sorry, I couldn't help overhearing. I certainly agree with you that Angela needs to be watched, but Julia has had her share of mishaps on this trip. I don't think it's a good idea for her to be hanging around with Angela."

"But someone should," Christof said. "And I cannot do it because I have to lead the group."

"I'll watch her," Dirk said. "I'm kind of eager to meet this elusive Gudrun."

"How can you do that? She's still afraid of you," I protested. "And it's nice to hear you don't want anything to happen to me."

He smiled. "I said I'd watch her, not attach myself to her with a leash. She won't even know it. But I can assure you, the second she speaks to someone outside our group, I'll be right there. And she's not going to wander off by herself anymore. As far as something happening to you, I doubt if I'm going to be able to stop you from doing stupid things, but at least there may not be blood and broken bones involved."

So what did his words mean? Was he trying to say he liked me?

"I have to tell you, Julia, I'm feeling extremely uneasy. For two cents I'd get off this damn bus and take the next flight home." Olivia rummaged in her bag and pulled out a container of Advil, a chocolate bar and a bottle of water.

"Me too, please," I said, stretching out my hand. "I'll bet my headache is worse than yours."

Olivia popped two pills into her mouth and washed them down. "I mean, how on earth is Angela doing all these crazy things? I'll bet she weighs close to two hundred pounds. There's no way in the world she can climb mountains or trees. And yet we always seem to find her in some impossible situation. It's downright spooky."

"I've been thinking about that," I told my friend. "She certainly isn't doing this alone. When she stood on the rock on the glacier, she really wasn't that high above the ground. Someone could have given her a hand up. Someone took her up the cliff at Vik. She said that much herself. But today and the tree?" I shook my head. "I have no idea how she managed that. And I keep thinking this Gudrun person has to be one of us, yet we're always all accounted for when Angela spots her elf. Today everyone was outside the shop waiting to board the bus. I know this because I was actually counting. Angela was the only one missing."

"Well, it gives me the creeps," Olivia said. "I can't wait to get out of here."

I agreed with her, but I wanted to show her something. "Angela has been stealing stuff from everyone so I'm guessing this doesn't belong to her. Have a look at this. It must have fallen out of Angela's pocket when she tumbled out of the tree."

It was a silver cigarette case with the initials LMB.

Olivia turned it over in her hand. "What a strange thing for Angela to have. And these are not her initials."

"Nope, they're not. I think they're the same initials that are on the little silver ball I found on the bus. As far as I can tell, Cameron is the only one who smokes, and he keeps a pack of Marlboros squashed in his jacket pocket. So, where did Angela get this? Or maybe a better question is why does she have it?"

When I saw Emma turn her head slightly in our direction, I put my finger to my lips and slipped the cigarette case back into my pocket. We'd have to wait for a better time to talk.

"I have arranged a special treat for you all this evening," Christof announced over his mic. "After we check into our hotel, we're going on a boat ride. Dinner will be served onboard, and if you are particularly adventurous, you can taste our live catch."

Oh, goody. More water.

CHAPTER FIFTEEN

Shortly after five o'clock we walked the short distance from the hotel to the dock. The others had already boarded the boat when Olivia and I arrived. We were delayed because she wasn't happy with her outfit, and I had a disastrous experience with eyeliner. It smudged under my eyes and wouldn't wash off, so now I had gray blotches accented with red from vigorous scrubbing. Certainly not the effect I was hoping for— not that anyone would notice.

The boat was wooden and old and creaked as it swayed at the dock. There was a small bar near the bow and a buffet and tables and chairs in the main cabin. Olivia and I bought glasses of wine and tried to mingle with the other passengers. The captain, an extremely hardy looking man with a ruddy face and full beard, told us we were the only group on board, and tonight was the last excursion of the season.

"I can't believe I dressed up for this," Olivia grumbled in my ear. "These are Escada jeans. When Christof said dinner on a boat, I assumed we were going to be on some kind of yacht. Not this old scow."

I rummaged through my shoulder bag looking for my sunglasses. Even though it was nearly dark, I wanted to hide my eyes.

"What's with the shades? It's almost night." Renee peered at me closely. "You look silly."

I resisted the urge to say, "Same to you." She was wearing blue satin cropped pants, so tight a panty line would have been clearly visible if she'd been wearing such a garment. A pink tube top, which she kept hoisting up, white six-inch heels and a pink sequin-studded headband completed the outfit. She had to be freezing. It was cold enough to see our breath, yet she looked like she was ready for a romp on the beach—or whatever. While I stammered something about the glare from the water hurting my eyes, Olivia said, "Planning on working tonight, Renee?"

Renee stuck her hand on her hip and said, "Huh?"

"Olivia, play nice," I warned my friend. Renee wasn't aware she looked like a hooker ready to work the room.

"I'm not teaching fitness tonight, if that's what you mean."

Olivia smiled benignly. "That's nice, dear. Let me know if you want to borrow my jacket." She pointed to Renee's chest. "You look cold."

Indeed, Renee's nipples poked at the fabric like two frozen mini marshmallows. I dragged my friend away before she said anymore and Renee figured out what she was talking about. We wandered into the main cabin where Christof was talking.

"If you go to the stern, you can see the crew bring up fresh seafood. You will be amazed at what they catch in their net."

Olivia and I pushed open the door to the aft deck and stepped into a blast of cold air. Cameron and Dirk were already watching as a crewmember lowered a net to the bottom of the sea. We greeted them pleasantly and took a place along the makeshift table so we could see what was going on. Dirk and Cameron seemed deep in conversation, and since Dirk didn't acknowledge me with more than a curt nod, I tried to ignore him. Ginger and George and the Bouchers were the only other folks brave enough to fight the howling wind.

The crewmember pulled up the net and dumped a load of crabs, sea urchins and scallops onto the table. Brandishing a knife, he said, "Who would like to try a scallop? I promise you they are sweet and delicious."

"Raw?" Olivia asked. "Without hollandaise?"

I agreed with my friend, but since Dirk already had several on his plate, I popped one into my mouth and chewed. It was surprisingly tender, and I took another.

"Now you're just showing off." She shook her head when the crewmember offered her a piece of sea urchin. "Let's go find something to eat that isn't still squiggling. Besides, this wind is wrecking my hair."

Suddenly Cameron began to wave his arms around and yell. "Tell them to stop the boat! I have to get off. I can't take it anymore."

Dirk put his arm around the shivering man. "Take it easy, friend. You're going to be fine," but Cameron was having none of it.

"I'm done!" he yelled. "There's no point tormenting me anymore! I don't know anything and I don't know what you want." He honestly looked like a crazy man. The wind had blown his hair into a wild mess, and in the darkening sky his face was ghostly pale.

"Why don't we go inside and talk about it?" Dirk urged. "Maybe have a beer." Dirk took the man's elbow and firmly led him into the cabin and away from our curious eyes and ears. Ginger and George, not wanting to miss any action, followed.

"Well," Olivia said, "I wonder what that was all about. Cameron sure did look upset. It sounded like someone was harassing him, but why would anybody do that?"

Nicole Boucher, who'd obviously heard the whole outburst, nodded in agreement. "The man's heading towards collapse. I've tried to get him to see a doctor, but he refuses. He keeps insisting he's okay. Serge offered to give him a sedative, but he said he can't afford to relax. In my opinion he can't afford not to."

"I feel sorry for him," I said. "This has to be a nightmare for the poor man."

She and I stood for a few minutes looking out at the blackness. Night had come quickly and the only light came from the ship's reflection on the water.

"She wasn't a nice person, you know." Her voice was so low I had to strain to hear her words. She shifted her eyes away from me and looked out at the sea. "Some people are naturally nasty. They're not satisfied with their own lives even when they seem to be perfect."

"Who are you talking about, Nicole? Do you mean Lydia?"

She nodded. "It's almost as if she came on this trip for a deliberate reason. Didn't you notice she never seemed interested in sightseeing?"

"I suppose I did notice," I said, "but people take these trips for many different reasons. Maybe she was trying something new—stepping out of her comfort zone." Personally, I didn't think Lydia was interested in anything but herself, but what did I know.

Nicole's voice hardened. "She came to harass my husband."

Oh, my! I looked around to see if anyone else was listening, but Olivia and Serge Boucher had gone in. And the crewmember was busy cleaning up the remains of the seafood.

"What makes you think that?" I asked. "And how would she go about doing it?"

"It's a long story."

"I have time. And the boat isn't going to dock for awhile." Fortunately, the wind was calming. It was still cold, but bearable without the frigid blasts.

Nicole leaned against the rail and said, "So it's like this. My husband performed a cardiac procedure on this elderly woman. He didn't really want to because she was pretty ill and fragile, but her family absolutely insisted. Well, it turned out badly. The woman died on the operating table. Her son blamed Serge for botching the surgery, even though he hadn't wanted to do it in the first place and had warned them of the risk."

"That is tough for your husband, but I don't see what that has to do with Lydia."

"I'm coming to that. The patient was Lydia's mother. Her brother is the one who insisted on the surgery. I don't know if you know this, but Lydia didn't come from money. She lived large, but her family sure didn't. I don't think she even liked her mother. One brother died in some kind of accident. The surviving brother shamed her into paying for the surgery because the family had no insurance. They kept telling her it was her duty as a daughter. When the mother died, the family blamed Lydia. They kept telling her the doctor was a quack and she shouldn't have let him operate. So naturally, Lydia turned her anger to my husband. She even took out ads in several California newspapers slandering him. Serge spent a fortune defending his reputation. I almost fainted when I saw her on this trip."

This was an amazing story. I, however, had a few questions. "I know Lark Tour gave all of us a list of fellow passengers before we left home. Didn't you see her name?"

"Nope. Back in those days she was still using Wilcox, which was her first husband's name. I read the list, but since I'd never heard of Lydia Cumberland, nothing jumped out at me."

Another distinctly unpleasant idea began to gnaw at me. "Dirk's from California. Sacramento, I believe. Did you know him? Or do you think he could have known Lydia?"

"I believe he's a well-known lawyer. I've seen articles about him defending high-powered clients. It's possible he could have read the slanderous stuff Lydia put in the papers, but I don't think he would connect her to the person on our trip. There would be no reason to do that."

She began to shiver, and I knew it was time to go inside. "One more question, Nicole," I said as I opened the door. "I'm curious if you perhaps knew Angela or Emma previously. Or Renee or Ginger? Maybe they had traveled on another trip with you?"

She paused. "There *is* something familiar about one of them. I just can't put my finger on it, but…"

"There you are, darling." Serge put his arm around his wife and hugged her. "I was wondering where you were." He shot me a look as he led his wife away.

What did he mean, he wondered where his wife was? He knew perfectly well she was on the aft deck with me because that's where he left her. Something really strange was going on.

Olivia stood with her arms folded, surveying our group. "These people are like vultures. Mention food and they claw to get to the head of the line."

I had to admit she was right. They arrived for every meal fifteen minutes early and plowed their way to the food as soon as the dining rooms opened. It was as if a starter gun went off, and everyone wanted to be first.

Olivia and I picked up plates and took our places at the end of the line. I passed up creamed corn and an unidentifiable meat in favor of potatoes and fish. As I reached for a hunk of bread, I smelled a familiar aftershave and felt someone standing next to me.

"Pardon my reach," Dirk said, extending his arm across me and snagging a roll. "That was pretty brave of you to eat the raw seafood." He smiled at me so I assumed we were being friendly.

"Do you want to sit with us?" I asked, pointing to seats at the end of the room.

"No, thanks. Renee asked me to eat with her. Skip is keeping Cameron company."

I glanced at Renee sitting prettily at a table. I noticed she had fluffed her hair and applied thicker layers of makeup. "I thought you were going to watch Angela," I said. "Shouldn't you be doing that?"

He looked amused. "I can see her from here, and as long as the boat's moving, I don't think she'll be able to climb a tree."

As he joined Renee, I watched her giggle at something he said. Then she whispered in his ear, which caused them both to laugh out loud. She even put her dainty little hand with the pointy talons on his shoulder and snuggled her cantaloupe-sized breasts against his arm. Right after that, she looked at me and wiggled her fingers in a wave. Suddenly I wasn't hungry anymore.

"I'm going outside," I said to Olivia. "I need some fresh air."

"You just had some." She glanced across the room, taking in the pair seated at the table. "Oh. I get it. You know, Julia, you really can't be upset about any of this. We're going home in a few days, and this is all going to be quickly forgotten."

"Righto." I didn't need a lecture from my friend. I needed to jump overboard and get away from these people. Once on the deck I leaned against the rail and took several deep breaths. Olivia was right—I was acting like an idiot. I obviously meant nothing to Dirk, and in a few days we were going to be on opposite sides of the country. And you know what they say. Out of sight, out of mind. Not that I was ever in his mind.

One thing was sure; I had no intention of going back into the cabin and mingling with the group. Let Renee make a fool of herself with Dirk. I hoped Skip would take his head off when he saw them together, although I didn't really think he cared. As I stood there, the lights from the shore came closer and I realized we were getting ready to dock which meant I'd soon have to be pleasant. That just wasn't going to work. I didn't want to talk to anyone and that included Olivia.

I remembered noticing a small bathroom right inside the cabin door. I'd looked in it before, hoping to use the facilities, but it was jammed with boxes and was obviously being used as a storeroom. It was perfect for my purpose, though. I would squeeze in there and wait until I heard the last passengers leave the boat, and then I would silently follow. Once in the bathroom, I pushed the boxes aside, lifted a heavy one marked "Life Jackets, Child," off the toilet lid and sat down.

I felt the boat thud gently against the pier and heard the captain tell folks to watch their step. I listened as everyone walked past my little hiding space. It seemed to take forever for their voices to fade away. When I heard a crewmember call to another to secure the rope in the bow, I figured it was time to leave. The others were far enough ahead of me. I would explain to Olivia later.

I stood up and turned the handle on the door. The handle moved down but nothing happened. I tried again, thinking it was stuck, but no luck. It wouldn't budge. I gave the door a shove. Still nothing. This was ridiculous. I banged—tentatively at first because I felt foolish—and then, when no one answered, harder. Soon I was pounding with both fists and instead of praying no one heard me, I prayed someone would. But no one did. The crew must have left the boat, and I was all alone.

I sat back down on the toilet and pulled my cell phone out of my bag. I would simply call Olivia and ask her to help me. I knew that even though she would raise her eyebrows in disapproval, she would somehow get me out and keep all the murky details to herself.

But there was no cell phone reception in the bathroom. I turned on the light bulb over the sink and saw my phone had no bars. I would have to think of something else. Surely, I reasoned, someone would miss me. When everyone arrived at the hotel, someone would say, "Where's good old Julia?" But who, exactly would say that? I hadn't endeared myself to most of my fellow travelers. But Olivia would be concerned. She would come looking for me.

For a minute my heart stopped bouncing like a basketball in my chest. Good old Olivia would be here in no time. But then, why would she come to the boat? Wouldn't she assume I got off with everyone else and was perhaps taking a stroll around the hotel? She knew I was upset. Maybe she'd think I wanted to be alone and therefore leave me alone. Would she simply go to our room and get ready for bed?

Now I was getting scared. And for some reason it was also getting hard to breathe. Was I hyperventilating? Maybe I was using up all the air in the little windowless room. It was also getting hot—steamy hot, and it wasn't my imagination. Sweat dripped from my eyes and ran down my body. I pulled my sweater over my head and tossed it into the sink.

I'd briefly attributed the sudden wave of heat that ran through my body to a panic attack or a hot flash, but for once I couldn't blame my body. It was definitely hot in that little room and getting hotter, and my internal thermostat had nothing to do with it. And I was still roasting. Without thinking I pulled off my T-shirt and wiped my face with it. My feet were soaked in my heavy walking shoes, so I kicked them off.

Now the room was hotter than a sauna. When I touched the faucet on the sink, I nearly burned my hand. Every breath I took felt like I was inhaling a searing blast of fire. I had to get out, but how? There was no window and repeated kicks at the door only resulted in a sore foot.

I wrapped my T-shirt around my hand and gingerly turned on the faucet in the sink. At first the water was hot, but when it gradually cooled, I soaked the shirt and wrapped it around my head. With that modicum of relief, I looked around the room, trying to figure out the source of the heat. Blasts of hot air seemed to be coming from a vent in the ceiling. Even standing on the toilet seat, it was out of my reach.

I couldn't stand this much longer. To add to my misery, my jeans were soaked from all the water I had splashed, and they clung uncomfortably to my legs. I peeled them down and wrestled them off my feet.

Every once in a while I pounded on the door and then listened intently, but there was no sound from outside. I could hear the boat creak as it bobbed gently against the dock, but that was all. Discouraged, I sat down on the toilet and put my head in my hands. By the time someone found me, I would be in a greasy puddle on the floor. A greasy, dead puddle. This time it seemed the person trying to do me in was going to succeed, because there was no doubt this was not an accident. Someone had barricaded the door from outside.

I lost track of time. I had no idea if hours or merely minutes had passed. I was desperately thirsty but the warm water from the sink made me gag, and the heat made me dizzy and sick to my stomach. I closed my eyes and tried to take shallow, even breaths.

I thought about Tony and our lunchroom and my cute little house and my dog, Barney. Barney was staying with my neighbor, Lottie Spenser. Would she be willing to keep him when she learned I was gone? Maybe Olivia would insist on taking him. I could hear her voice now. She sure was yelling. Maybe Barney was lost—except she wasn't calling Barney. She was calling my name. I opened my eyes and listened. I wasn't dreaming or about to stroll through the Pearly Gates. Olivia was on the boat and she was looking for me.

I got to my feet and banged with all my strength on the door. I almost wept when I heard her voice come nearer, then fade.

"Wait!" I yelled. "Don't go. I'm in here!" Thank God I heard her voice return. "Olivia, let me out!"

All at once, the door banged open and without waiting for pleasantries, I raced out and took deep gulps of the cold night air. Then I put my hands on my thighs and heaved until my stomach was empty.

"Hey! You just threw up on my Jimmy Choos!"

When I finally looked up, Olivia stood in front of me with her hands on her hips. And next to her stood Dirk. He smiled. "You seem to have a problem keeping your clothes on."

I was suddenly acutely aware they were dressed for arctic weather and I was soaking wet in my underwear. Olivia stepped into the bathroom and quickly reappeared holding my sodden clothes and shoes.

"It's hotter than hell in there. Hotter than a sauna. And she has no clothes to wear."

Dirk took off his jacket and put it around my shoulders. "Put this on. And zip it up. It's cold out there. You're going to have to wear your shoes. I don't think mine would fit you. Will you ladies excuse me for a minute? There's something I want to check."

I bent down and squashed my feet into my sodden shoes. He sure wasn't kidding about the temperature. It was so cold my clacking teeth sounded like castanets. "How did you know where I was?" I asked as we quickly climbed off the boat and hurried down the dock.

"I hunted for you everywhere," Olivia said. "I finally got worried when I couldn't find you at the hotel and all the cafes were closed. I didn't know what to do so I called Dirk and he suggested we go back to the boat."

"Did he, now?" I sounded snarky but I'd been nanoseconds away from collapsing into a lifeless heap on the ground, and someone was going to pay. "Why would he think of looking for me on the boat?"

"Don't do that, Julia," Olivia warned. "You're lucky we found you. Somebody had wedged a board against the door. You'd never have been able to get out by yourself."

We waited by the dock until Dirk caught up with us. I intended to ignore him, but Olivia wanted to chat. "What were you doing back there? Did you find anything interesting?"

"Enough to make me know someone is trying to harm Julia. The thermostat on the boat was turned up as high as it would go. Interestingly enough, there's only one heat vent in the main cabin and another two in the restrooms. The vent in the cabin was closed, which made the little room Julia was stuck in mighty hot. You wouldn't have died," he said to me, "but you could have been very sick.

At the moment, I didn't want to rehash the whole episode. I just wanted to get back to the hotel and get warm. I was freezing.

"Is there a taxi or something?" I asked. I was shivering so violently I could hardly speak.

"Julia, the hotel is right up there," Olivia said, pointing to a building ahead of us on the hill. Come on, you can make it."

Dirk tried to take my arm but I shook him off. "I can walk by myself, thank you."

"Sorry. I was only trying to hold you up. You seem to be wobbling a bit."

"I'm not," I assured him. "But thank you for caring. This is the way I normally walk."

"Really? I never noticed."

"You apparently haven't noticed a lot of things."

"People!" Olivia exclaimed. "Let's get back to the hotel and get Julia into some dry clothes. Then you can hurl barbs if you want to."

"I'd rather throw something heavier," I said under my breath, but Dirk heard me. I knew this because he said, "And I feel like throwing you in the water, although you're already wet, so it wouldn't cool you off. If I didn't think you were in some kind of shock from your recent experience, I'd gladly leave you alone."

I tried to march ahead, but the wet running shoes squished as I walked, ruining the whole indignation thing. I was scared, cold and shivering and had no idea how I was going to get through the hotel lobby without answering a barrage of questions.

At the entrance, Dirk solved this problem by scooping me up and carrying me through the crowded reception area. He shot a terse "bit of a stomach upset" to the desk clerk, who jumped away, eager to avoid any errant germs.

Olivia unlocked the door to our room and Dirk dumped me on my bed. "When you're dry and in a better mood, we need to talk. Let me know."

CHAPTER SIXTEEN

As soon as he was gone, I crawled off the bed and went into the bathroom to survey the damage. As I expected, I looked awful. My hair, which frizzes when it's wet, hung around my head like squiggling snakes, and my face was the color of a tomato. Olivia stood anxiously at the door and surveyed the wreckage that was me.

"This is serious, Julia. Something evil is going on here. Someone is trying to hurt you."

"You think?" I quickly pulled on clean underwear, jeans and a sweater. I toweled my hair dry and tried to comb it, but the teeth of the comb were no match for the steel wool it was trying to tame.

"So do we find Dirk now?" Olivia actually wrung her hands. "I think he means we need to talk tonight."

"I'm not going to his room again," I yelled. "I don't care what he wants."

"Well, I want to get home in one piece. I think he can offer some help—certainly security."

"Olivia, how do you know *he* didn't bar the door?" I gave up trying to fix my hair and clamped a baseball cap on my head. "From this point on, I trust no one."

"He couldn't have barred the door. He walked back to the hotel with Skip, Renee and me. And he was right ahead of us getting off the boat. I would have seen him if he'd tweaked a thermostat. I don't know where the rest of our group was, but I know for sure Dirk didn't do it. And I think we should hear what he has to say."

I swiped blush across my cheeks and stomped out the door. "Go get him. But tell him we'll meet in the lobby or somewhere public. I'll wait."

Olivia looked at me as if she was conversing with the Mad Hatter, but she hurried out of the room before I could tell her I'd changed my mind. I leaned against the wall and closed my eyes, trying to remember if I'd heard anything that would tell us who was after me. As we were docking, I'd heard the voices of the crew telling everyone to watch their steps. And then the voices had faded and I'd stayed quiet until I was sure there was no one around. I replayed the memory in my mind. I remembered sitting on the edge of the toilet and pulling the scarf off my neck and stuffing it into my pocket. When I couldn't hear any more sounds, I stood up and was about to open the door. But I hesitated. What made me do that? A muffled giggle? Now I remembered. It was soft and low and not meant to be heard, but since I was straining to hear every sound on the boat, I heard it. Was it someone exiting the boat? I had no time to think about it now because Olivia knocked lightly on the door and asked, "Are you decent?" I pulled the door open and glared at her. "Of course I am. Why wouldn't I be?"

"Then let's go. Per your instructions, we're going to have our chat in the lobby, although it won't be very private."

I swung into the hall and marched to the elevator, barely glancing at Dirk, who looked sensational in khaki pants and a blue and green striped shirt.

"Glad to see you feel okay," he said, easily keeping up with me. "That had to have been a very unpleasant experience."

The three of us rode the elevator to the lobby in awkward silence, and as soon as we stepped out, I knew I'd made a mistake. The couches and chairs in the small seating area were occupied. Our only option was to sit at the bar. George Reilly was there, too, and he sure wasn't sober.

"Hell of a trip, isn't it?" His words were so slurred, he was hard to understand. "One of us killed that bitch. The thing is, which one? Interesting question, isn't it?" His glazed eyes stared at us. "Maybe one of you whacked her. I wouldn't have minded doing it myself. Couldn't stand the bitch. She had a wicked tongue. It's good someone shut her up."

As he lurched towards us, his elbow knocked his beer glass onto the counter. I watched in dismay as the golden liquid dripped onto my lap. When George picked up a napkin and clumsily tried to sop up the mess, I jumped to my feet and pushed his hand away. I wanted to tell him he should stop making such inflammatory remarks, but the beer was seeping through the fabric of my jeans, and I decided I didn't care if folks heard his words.

"I'm leaving," I said to Dirk. "I've had enough for one day."

He stood up and followed Olivia and me out of the bar. "Let's go outside, and don't worry about your pants. It's not as if this is the first time your clothes have been wet."

He tried to take my arm, but I pulled away. "I'll walk if you stop trying to guide me. I'm perfectly capable of moving on my own."

He ignored me. "I have something to tell you both, but you have to keep it to yourselves. Promise me?"

"Absolutely," Olivia said.

I pursed my lips and nodded. The three of us walked along the deserted path in front of the hotel. In the moonlight the twisted branches of the trees looked spooky. I found myself hoping there was no truth to Angela's stories about trolls and hidden people.

"I learned something interesting," Dirk said. "Would you like to hear what it is?"

"Certainly," Olivia said. I thought she sounded a little breathless.

"Julia?" When I didn't answer, he said, "Do you want to hear?"

"Oh, for heavens sake, stop being so juvenile. If you know something important, spit it out. Otherwise I'm going back."

He laughed. "Okay. Since you asked so nicely, I'll tell you. I managed to get some information from the police in Reykjavik. They haven't completely finished the autopsy yet, but they know how Lydia died. Strictly speaking, she wasn't killed from falling down the glacier." He paused. "She had ingested a large quantity of drugs."

"What!" The words burst out of me. "But how is that possible? Wouldn't we have noticed if she'd been under the influence of something? Personally, I thought she could have benefited from some kind of mood equalizer. She always seemed too sharp-tongued. Too crisp."

"According to the police, she had enough drugs in her to make her very sick. They even suggested it might have been a suicide. They think she was unconscious when she fell down the side of the glacier. She hit her head—there was a large bump on the side of her skull—and died. The drug they found is ketamine. It's used to treat bipolar conditions or to put someone to sleep before surgery. It's also now being used to treat depression, but large overdoses can cause death.

They interviewed Cameron, and he told them as far as he knew the only medication she took was a statin for high cholesterol. This tour will soon be over, and I think the police are satisfied with the drug explanation.

They don't want to get involved in suspicious deaths with foreigners."

I looked at him skeptically. "Are we? Satisfied, that is? George and Angela are already running around crying murder."

"No. I don't think we are. There are too many unanswered questions—like who is Gudrun and why has someone been trying to hurt you, Julia? Plus, there were no drugs found in Lydia's belongings. Someone gave it to her deliberately. I think someone wanted her dead."

"So who would have access to this ketamine?" I asked. "Nicole and Serge? An ex-nurse and a doctor? Those two could easily get that stuff."

"I'll bet Emma takes mood enhancers," Olivia said. "And I know she drinks because I've seen her sip from her flask when she thinks no one's watching. And Angela? She seems like a likely candidate. Who else?"

"There's no way of knowing," Dirk said. "No one's going to chat about depression or being bipolar. But we're forgetting one major thing. If Lydia was murdered, someone had the means and a very strong motive for killing her. We just have to figure out what that was."

I cleared my throat, which had suddenly become dry. "What if George had been drugged with the same stuff? He said he found candy outside his door. Maybe it had ketamine in it."

"Why would anyone want to kill George?" Olivia asked.

I suddenly realized I was cold—whether from the conversation or the chilly air I didn't know—but I wanted to go back to the hotel and bury myself under my pillow.

"Time to go," I said. "Well, have fun solving this."

Dirk's voice cut through the night. "Julia, like it or not, you are involved. Someone—probably the murderer—is convinced you *know* something. We just have to figure out what that is. It could be something you heard or saw. Something that meant nothing to you." His voice softened. "This isn't a criticism, but you do tend to speak your mind. Whatever it is has alarmed the killer enough to want to, well...let's just say we need to figure this out, and the sooner the better."

"I'm in," Olivia whispered.

"Julia?"

"I want to go home. I've had enough."

His voice softened. "Has the trip really been that awful?"

I narrowed my eyes and squinted at him in the darkness. So he hadn't forgotten. Was he actually going to mention whatever-it-was in front of Olivia?

"It's been pretty awful, but it may have had its moments," I said.

Olivia coughed delicately.

"I particularly enjoyed the lecture on geothermal energy," he said, grinning. "Didn't you?"

"I don't want to talk to you anymore. Let's go, Olivia. We need to get to sleep so we're ready for another fun-filled day. Can't wait to see what new terror awaits me."

Although after I read the itinerary I decided I could—wait, that is. Tomorrow we were visiting a horse farm, and I decided to stay as far away as possible from anything with hooves that could stampede. I didn't want to hear Angela say hidden people spooked them.

CHAPTER SEVENTEEN

The bus wound its way up a long gravel drive and stopped in front of a series of low white buildings. A trim blond woman met us as we clambered down the steps. She looked fit and healthy, dressed in a short black skirt, tights and boots. A gray, three-quarter sleeve sweater covered a black top.

"Welcome. I am Katrin and this is my daughter, Stefania," she said, indicating a dark-haired girl standing next to her and holding the reins of a horse. "We will take you on a brief tour of the farm and then serve a lunch we hope you will enjoy. Please follow me."

"This seems harmless enough," I whispered to Olivia. "I'm not getting close to any of them though, and I'm hanging onto you."

"This is a twenty-three thousand acre horse farm," Katrin told us. "It has been in my family for over one hundred years. We raise Icelandic horses, which you will have a chance to see in action."

Once again I marveled at the stark beauty and vastness of Iceland. A cloud formed a perfect circle around the mountain behind the farm, leaving only the peak visible. In the morning sunlight, the pristine white buildings with the red roofs, the emerald grass and bright blue sky looked like objects in a lovely painting.

This place was so isolated, I wondered what people did for fun. Or where they shopped for food. Or found a doctor. But Kristin looked happy and healthy and well nourished, so I decided folks here must thrive in the crisp pure air.

Our group dutifully trooped after our host, which gave me a chance to count noses. We were all there. Emma linked arms with her husband and Cameron and chattered happily about cloud formations. The Bouchers tried without luck to check their cell phones for messages. The Twins and Skip stopped to watch a horse being put through its paces in the pasture. Every few feet Angela stooped to pick up something and put it in a plastic bag.

"What do you think she's doing?" I asked Olivia.

"Who knows. She's batty enough to be picking up horse manure, so I believe I'll stay away from her."

Ahead of us, Dirk walked with Renee. I watched her rub up against his arm and look up at him adoringly. She reminded me of a cat. I expected him to move away, but instead he laughed and put his arm around her shoulder. What the heck! Where was Skip when you needed him!

"How can he possibly be enjoying that?" I said to Olivia. "Men are so stupid."

"Are you kidding? He'd have to be a eunuch to move away. I am, however, wondering what her husband would think."

"Or why he isn't here." I shifted my eyes to a figure moving rapidly towards us. "Ah, here he comes now. And he doesn't look very happy."

Indeed, he didn't. "I hope Skip is smart enough not to tangle with Dirk," I said. "Sure, Skip is younger and has some impressive muscles, but I have a feeling he wouldn't last long in a fight." Secretly, though, I hoped Skip would flatten him.

I watched as Skip grabbed his wife's arm and tried to pull her away. Dirk put up his hand like a traffic cop and her husband instantly let go.

At that moment, Katrin stopped walking and called, "Please follow me into the house. We have prepared a delicious lunch for you."

We stepped into an inviting dining room with two long wooden tables in the middle. Three young girls with blond hair said, "Please sit. Mama will bring the food soon."

Olivia and I hung back, hoping to avoid sitting next to Angela or Renee or Emma. We thought we were safe when we slid into chairs at the end of a table, but as soon as we sat down, Emma plopped into the chair next to me.

"I must say, I've never done so much walking. I wish I had my cane."

I smiled politely and looked around for help, but Olivia was talking to the Bouchers.

"I'm glad I have you alone," Emma began. "There's something I need to tell you."

Oh boy! "What is it, Emma? I certainly have enjoyed your copious notes. Have I forgotten to thank you?"

She dismissed my words with a wave of her hand. "Yes, yes. Well, I mean, no, you haven't thanked me, but right now that doesn't concern me—although I must say, Julia, you can be a very abrupt person."

I waited, knowing there would be more. She fiddled with the tassels on her skirt and said, "I know something that might be important. I'm only going to tell you this because your husband was a detective so I'm thinking you might have some kind of listening or deducting skills."

"My husband wasn't a detective. He was a cop and…"

"Please don't interrupt me, Julia." She ran her hand nervously through her hair. "I have to talk fast. Someone might come and I won't be able to finish."

She took a deep breath and plunged ahead. "Remember when you asked if I'd ever seen any of our passengers on other trips? I didn't exactly answer truthfully." Her eyes darted around the room. "It wasn't a Lark tour. It was with another company and there were loads of guests. I only remember her because she was so flamboyant. Just like she is today."

It didn't require rocket science to figure out whom she meant. "I assume you're talking about Renee?"

She put her finger to her lips. "Shh. We don't need to tell the others. It was Renee. At least I'm pretty sure it was. But she was with someone else. Not Skip. He was another muscle bound creature with huge biceps." She sniffed. "She seems to go for that type. Anyway, they always made a big show of being together. I think public displays of affection are revolting. Nathan and I would never do that."

I waved my hand impatiently. "I'm sure you wouldn't. Keep talking. This is very interesting. Do you think she recognizes you on this trip?"

Emma shook her head. "I'm sure she doesn't. I wasn't traveling with Nathan. I was with three ladies from my book club. Renee never glanced at us."

"And you're sure the man she was with wasn't Skip?"

"Positive. He was the same type, but he had blond hair, and I'm pretty sure he spoke with an accent. But there's much more I have to tell you."

I figured we had maybe five minutes left until Katrina reached us with the food. She had already entered the room and was serving folks at the other table.

"Talk fast, Emma. What else have you got?"

"On the passenger list for that trip, Renee listed her home as San Francisco, not Akron." She paused to let that information sink in. "Don't you see? She could have known Lydia. Maybe she was blackmailing her or something."

"Would you happen to remember this person's last name?"

Emma shook her head. "It was a very large list. I only remember her first name was Tangerine, which I totally felt suited such a floozy. I remembered she was from California because I thought it was unusual for her to be on the east coast to begin the tour. Our trip went to Japan."

"Maybe her traveling companion lived on the east coast. Are you absolutely sure it was Renee? There are a lot of flashy women in the world. You might be mistaken."

She gave me a smug smile. "What would you say if I told you I had proof?"

"I'd say let's hear it. And fast because the food is almost here."

"You're so impatient, Julia. It was like this. I was passing Skip and Renee's room in the hotel and noticed the door was slightly ajar, so, of course, I was concerned. You can't be too careful in these foreign countries, you know. I was going to pull it shut when I saw Renee's tote bag right there on the bed." She shook her head. "That's so careless. Anyone could walk in and take it."

I struggled to keep my eyebrows from crawling across my forehead. Our Emma had been snooping. And she sounded so pious about it.

"Well. I certainly couldn't leave without doing *something*. By the way, Renee has an impressive assortment of vitamins and herbal tonics. I suppose that stuff helps her look so young. Anyway, I walked over to the bed, intending to put the bag somewhere safe, perhaps in the bathroom, but as soon as I picked it up, her wallet and passport fell out. I glanced at the wallet and passport—just to make sure they were hers before I stuck them back in."

She saw the look on my face and said, "I wasn't going through her things. I simply wanted to make sure the bag belonged to Renee."

Emma, Emma, Emma! The woman had no shame. I made a mental note to keep my luggage locked.

"Anyway, I discovered something very interesting," she continued. "Can you guess what the lovely Renee's real name is?"

It was a rhetorical question because she nearly shouted the answer. "It's Tangerine! And that was the name of the person on the trip. What are the odds two people would look like that and have the same name?"

I had to admit the odds weren't great.

"Do you want to know what else I'm thinking?"

"Might as well tell me," I said.

"Your special friend, Dirk, is from California. Maybe he knew Renee. You have to admit they'd make a splendid couple. Maybe they had an affair and Lydia found out and threatened to tell Skip."

"First of all, he's not my special friend. And second, California is a big state, so it's highly unlikely he would know Renee. And why would Lydia care if they had an affair? It doesn't make any sense."

"I saw the way those two looked at each other on the boat. And today they certainly seemed cozy walking together. I think it's just terrible we have to travel with someone like that. Such lax morals. Who knows what they both are capable of doing?"

"Emma, please! You have no idea what you're talking about, and it's dangerous to have such wild theories."

I hoped she would at least look chagrined, but she patted her hair and smiled. "I don't expect you to agree with me, Julia. After all, you, too, are having a little fling with the handsome Dirk, are you not?"

"Well, I certainly am not," I sputtered. "Where did you even get such an idea?" Good grief! Was the woman looking through keyholes now?

CHAPTER EIGHTEEN

After a satisfying lunch of salmon, little red potatoes and crisp, fresh carrots and beans, Katrina invited us outside for a demonstration of Icelandic horses. I waited until the others in our group filed out of the dining room. My new motto was to keep everyone in front of me where I could keep an eye on them. But as soon as we stepped outside, several scattered in different directions. I watched Cameron head toward the bus—probably to smoke a cigarette—along with Emma and Nathan. I didn't think Emma was interested in a smoke. I strongly suspected she was more interested in enjoying a nip from her flask. She would probably call it a "digestif," but more than once I saw her hastily stow a bottle in her bag and reach for the breath mints.

As my eyes scanned the beautiful horse farm, I noticed a half-built structure with a large bolder in front of it. Curious, I asked Katrina what it was.

"Ah, yes," she said, shading her eyes with her hand. "That was going to be a new barn especially for boarding. We need the space, you see. We have many guests requesting to bring their own horses. Work was going well until the foreman ordered that big boulder removed. All of a sudden, bad things began to happen. One worker fell off a ladder and broke his foot. Another said his wife was filing for divorce." She frowned. "We could probably have overcome these things, but then the foreman's daughter gave birth to a baby with webbed feet, and well...that was too much. The workers blamed the elves living in the rock for all the trouble and refused to move it. They said the elves were angry and didn't want their home disturbed. There was nothing we could do."

Oh boy! Elves living in a rock. I hoped Angela hadn't heard any of this, but of course, she had. She was behind me, and from the look on her face, I could tell she was excited.

"The hidden folk must be so upset. I must try to speak to them."

"No, you don't," I warned. "Stay with the group and don't get into trouble. We all worry when you wander off."

But it was like talking to a guppy. She paid no attention to me and sped off in the direction of the unfinished barn. Sighing, I fell back and waited for Dirk to catch up with me.

"I thought you were going to watch her," I said, pointing to Angela's receding figure.

"I'm watching. She can't get into much trouble here. I don't see any tree to climb." He looked amused, as if he were talking to a cranky child.

"Okay, then," I said stiffly. "I'm glad you have everything under control." It was meant to sound sarcastic, but I could tell Dirk wasn't listening.

By now, Angela had reached the structure. "She can't get in," Katrina informed us. The entrance is barricaded to prevent accidents."

This was hardly consoling. Our host didn't know our Angela.

Since the rest of the group was still with us, we followed our host to a grassy riding ring. A man dressed in dark jeans, a black jacket with a helmet on his head held the reins of a small dark brown horse with a shaggy mane.

"This is my husband," Katrina said. "He will give you an exhibition of the skills of our wonderful Icelandic horses. Those of you familiar with riding will notice our horses have five gaits: the normal walk, trot, canter and gallop, plus a fifth one—the tolt. For the tolt, a horse always has either one or two feet on the ground. Our horses do this naturally. You can often see young foals tolt in the fields. This gait gives a very smooth ride, which means the rider can go long distances without tiring. Watch my husband as he puts Dyggur into the tolt. See how smooth it is?"

Used to much statelier horses back home, it at first seemed odd to see a tall man sitting proudly on the back of a small horse, but the performance was magical. It was if the horse moved on a cloud of air over the ground.

As I watched, I felt myself relax. The lunch had been delicious, the sun was warm and the lovely peaceful setting made me feel far removed from any danger. I even forgot to keep track of the rest of the group. When I looked around, the only people in sight were Angela and Emma—and they were huddled together in earnest conversation. I walked up to them and tapped Emma on the shoulder.

"So what are you talking about?"

Emma put her finger to her lips, but Angela blurted out, "Emma has seen Gudrun."

I gave Emma what I hoped was a piercing glance. "Really, Emma? When did this happen?"

"I know you don't believe in the *huldufólk*. That's why I didn't tell you."

Lordy! Not another one! It was bad enough to have Angela ranting about hidden people, but we didn't need Emma doing it, too.

"Stop this nonsense," I said softly to Emma. "You know perfectly well you haven't seen Gudrun or any other troll."

"Oh, but I have," she said smugly. "And they aren't trolls. They are hidden people. You're just upset because Angela doesn't take you into her confidence."

"I'm upset because something very evil is happening here, someone is responsible for it, and whoever it is sees nothing wrong with tormenting an already unbalanced woman. I'm talking about your friend here," I said, pointing to Angela, who was pulling tissues out of her bag and throwing them on the ground.

During my little speech, Emma's face turned several shades of red. She drew herself up to her full five feet and said, "I assure you I'm not making this up. I have seen Gudrun."

"Was she dressed as an elf? Did you meet her in a tree?"

"Certainly not. She was dressed like everyone else. As I recall, she wore a hoody and black pants. And sunglasses."

"Where exactly did this happen? And what did she say?"

"I saw them together at the black beach." She hesitated and looked at the ground. "Maybe I didn't exactly speak to her. But I certainly saw her. She was talking to Angela."

I was unimpressed. "How do you know it was Gudrun? It could have been another visitor to the beach. And if the figure was wearing a hoody and sunglasses, how do you know it was even a woman?"

"You think you're so smart, Julia, but you're really not. I'm sure it was Gudrun."

I knew I'd regret asking this question, but I did anyway. "How can you be so sure?"

"Because, Miss Know-It-All, I yelled 'Gudrun, may I speak with you for a minute?' and she shook her head and ran back home to the rock."

Lordy! I was getting a headache. "She went into a rock?"

"Well, I didn't exactly see her go into it. She went behind it. I think the entrance was in the back."

I'd had enough of Emma, Angela and people living in rocks. I needed to find the others. "Do you know where the rest of the group is?"

Angela shrugged, but Emma couldn't wait to tell me. "Renee and your friend, Dirk, are in the barn." She pointed across the grass to the half-finished structure. "I saw them go in a while ago, and they haven't come out yet."

Swell.

I walked across the grass, mentally concocting a reason for visiting the barn. I would simply say I was looking for Nicole and Serge. As I approached, I noticed someone had pulled boards away from the entrance—no doubt by Angela, who seemed to have superhuman strength. I stumbled through overgrown weeds and stepped gingerly into the dark interior. As my eyes adjusted to the light, I saw spaces had been created for a tack room. I knew stalls were intended for each side of the center aisle, but right now it was empty, cold, cavernous and dark. As I stood there, I heard voices coming from somewhere at the end of the barn. I cautiously walked toward the sounds, aware that my heart was beating so loudly, the folks would probably hear me coming. I felt like someone had punched me in the stomach when I heard a familiar laugh. It was unmistakable, annoying, and it came from Renee—or Tangerine, as I now intended to call her.

They were sitting on wooden crates, and their heads were so close together, it was difficult to determine what they were doing. For the sake of my sanity, I assumed they were talking. Dirk seemed startled to see me, but I watched a smug smile spread over Tangerine's face.

"Are you looking for someone?" she asked.

I felt the blood rush to my face as I stammered, "Sorry. I thought Angela and Emma might be here, and I was worried Angela was chasing hidden people again."

Dirk looked amused. "I told you I'd keep an eye on her."

"So you did. And I can see you're doing that." My words sounded snarky, but I didn't care.

Tangerine stood up and extended her hand to Dirk. "Come on. I'll buy you a drink. They must have wine or something at the house."

I was disgusted to see Dirk follow her like an obedient puppy. As she passed me, she said, "Sorry, honey. You don't stand a chance with him."

As if I wanted one!

"You're awfully quiet this evening."

Tonight was our home-hosted dinner. Our bus had brought us up a steep road to a white multi-level house built into a hillside. As we walked down the winding path to the door, we had a spectacular view of the lights of Akureyri below.

"I guess I don't have much to say," I told Olivia. I couldn't get the image of Dirk and Tangerine sitting together out of my mind. For some reason, I never thought he was the sort of man who would be attracted to a married woman. But why wouldn't he be? I kept telling myself I hardly knew the man, and in a few days I'd never, ever see him again. I needed to forget about him and our stupid indiscretion in his room. But that was hard to do when he put his arm around my shoulder and said, "This is quite a house, isn't it?"

Even though I didn't feel like speaking to him, I had to admit it was. The rooms weren't large, but they were warmly lit and furnished in the clean, functional furniture so typical in Iceland. Pillows and throws added colorful accents. The wooden trestle table was laden with smoked salmon, herring prepared in several different ways, big baskets of bread, and bowls of raw carrots, cauliflower and broccoli. So far on this trip the menus hadn't been extensive, but the food sure was good. Very healthy.

I had to push thoughts of food out of my mind because I was acutely aware of Dirk's warm hand on my shoulder. I kept reminding myself I didn't care about him, and he was truly a snake for sniffing around a married woman. Not that he was actually sniffing. I was pretty sure he was doing more than that.

Since I seemed to be mute, Olivia said, "I'm so tired of eating things that are good for me. I'm sick of fish. I'm craving something fried with grease and mayonnaise."

I picked up a plate and filled it with slices of salmon and veggies. "Think about how happy your body must be. It's probably wondering what in the world has happened."

Olivia scowled. "Very funny. I just don't think I can digest this stuff anymore. My stomach isn't used to all this roughage."

"If you ladies could stop discussing intestines and fiber for a few minutes, I'd like to talk to both of you." Dirk nodded his head toward a couch. "We can sit there."

I hated to follow his orders, but I wanted to hear what he had to say, so I trotted behind him across the room. Olivia sat down at one end of the sofa, forcing me to sit next to him.

His eyes scanned the room. "I don't think anyone is paying any attention to us. If we speak softly, we should be okay."

"Okay for what?" I stabbed a piece of fish and stuck it in my mouth. "I've been feeling okay all along."

Dirk looked at me curiously. "I don't know what's the matter with you, but we really don't have time to talk about it. I have some info I want to share with you." When I didn't answer, he said, "I've been trying to get close to Renee."

"So I've noticed." Darn! I needed to staple my lips shut.

"I'm going to ignore that because, again, I don't know what's up with you." He looked across me at Olivia. "I've been talking to Renee because she had casually mentioned she had at some time worked for a pharmaceutical company. Since Lydia Cumberland had a large amount of ketamine in her system, I thought Renee might be worth a closer look."

So that's why he was so interested in Tangerine! He wasn't after her totally willing body. I surreptitiously eyed her across the room. Blond hair in a high ponytail, black cropped pants that appeared to be sprayed on, and a purple fuzzy top with a sweetheart neckline. And buckets of makeup. She looked like a hooker—and who was I kidding—a man would have to be a eunuch not to be attracted. Still, Dirk was sitting here with us and not drooling all over her. I sat up straighter and attempted a smile.

"That *is* interesting information."

Dirk agreed. "It has also occurred to me that you're probably right about George being drugged. I mean, why would someone leave a bag of candy outside his door?" If it were part of the tour program, wouldn't we all have received one? Also—and this is just a theory—but what if the candy wasn't meant for George? What if the person who left it was confused about room numbers?" His eyes became hard. "What if it was intended for you, Julia?"

I gulped. "I don't much like that theory"

"You know what this means," Olivia said. "It means someone on this trip has a quantity of this stuff hidden somewhere."

My fingers suddenly felt like popsicles. "Boy, I can't wait for this trip to end. All I want to do is go home."

"Since we can't do that for a few days, I suggest we try to figure out exactly what we know—and who could be the one..." His voice trailed off. "You both know what I was going to say."

For a few minutes we sat in silence. I looked around the room at the rest of our group, wondering who among us could possibly be so evil. No one seemed like a killer. The Bouchers sat with Christof. As far as I could tell, they were eating and having a friendly conversation. Emma and Nathan stood at the buffet table—Nathan acting as a shield as Emma stuffed rolls into her big bag. Embarrassing for her if she was caught but hardly a crime. Skip and George stood in a corner drinking beer. I didn't see Ginger and assumed she was in the ladies room. Tangerine flitted from group to group, never totally taking her eyes off Dirk. Angela stood by herself, talking to a painting of a man on a horse.

Over the past two weeks I'd come to know these people pretty well, and it was hard to imagine one of them was a murderer. But fact is fact. And if we wanted to get home in a vertical position, we had to do something. So I said, "Maybe someone should search their rooms."

"Don't look at me." Olivia stood up. "I'm going to get some dessert and pretend I didn't hear that."

As soon as Olivia vacated her place on the couch, I saw Tangerine make a beeline for it, but Dirk must have given her some kind of look because she stopped and pretended to look out a window.

Dirk stared at me. "That's a dumb idea."

"Do you have a better one? One of us is running around with a substance capable of killing. What better way to find it than to look for it?"

"If this weren't a really stupid idea, how would you propose doing it?"

"Why all of a sudden am I the one doing the searching? What's wrong with you?"

He put his plate on an end table and leaned back on the couch. "Let's just say I somehow managed to search some of our guests' luggage—which I assume is what you're proposing. What if, just as I reach into, say Emma's suitcase, I'm caught with her panties in my hand. How would that look?"

At the mention of panties, I felt my cheeks turn crimson. This was not lost on Dirk, who tried hard not to smile. "People might think I had some kind of underwear fetish."

He needed to stop talking about underwear. Right now.

"You, on the other hand, would probably be able to come up with a logical explanation. But I have to say I think the whole idea is silly—and dangerous."

I hated it when someone told me not to do something. It reinforced my resolve to do whatever it was. So naturally, I stood up and announced, "Tomorrow morning I will search some rooms when people are at breakfast. Not all the rooms, but some of the more likely candidates."

He shook his head. "I think you're crazy, but that may be part of your charm."

Suddenly I felt my ears burn.

"Would you be willing to tell me which rooms you plan to examine? And would you please share how you intend to get into them? I'm worried you're going to do something totally illegal."

"I don't know yet which rooms, but when I figure it out I'll let you know. As far as how I intend to gain entrance—that is a professional secret."

That was something he really didn't need to know.

CHAPTER NINETEEN

"This is what we'll do. Christof always assembles us after breakfast in the lobby before the day's adventure. If we skip breakfast, we should have plenty of time."

Olivia looked doubtful. "How are we going to explain our absence? Isn't attendance almost mandatory?"

"We can fake some kind of stomach bug. That always happens to people traveling. No one will question it."

"Both of us are sick? Isn't that unlikely?"

"I don't know, Olivia. Maybe we went into town and ate tainted hot dogs. Work with me here. I don't have a better plan. It's now or never."

Olivia finished applying mascara and brushed blush on her cheeks. After a swipe of gloss on her lips, she said, "I actually do have a better plan. I'll go down to the dining room and case the joint. I'll say you aren't feeling well and don't want breakfast. If you tell me which rooms you want to search, I'll be able to tell you if their occupants are eating."

This plan actually made a lot of sense. "I'm thinking the Bouchers because of their medical association, Emma and Nathan because I'm dying to see what's in her big bag and Skip and Tangerine mostly because I don't like her and am hoping to find a vat of drugs so she can go to jail. We'll see how she likes wearing a baggy orange jumpsuit."

Olivia pulled on jeans and a yellow sweater. "It would probably be better if we kept emotions out of it.

I'm going down now. You figure out how you're going to get into the rooms."

The hotel was old and the locks on the doors were simple key locks. No fancy cards to stick in slots and no deadbolts. And I knew how to deal with those locks because Tony had taught me many years ago. This skill came under the heading of Useful Knowledge—along with how to change a tire, how to get out of a chokehold and how to turn a belt into handcuffs. I had humored my husband because I loved him, but at the time thought this was useless knowledge. Now, not so much.

After Olivia left, I assembled my lock-picking tools. Fortunately, my friend had long hair that she loved to pile on top of her head. This up-do required several sturdy pins to anchor it in place. I grabbed a few of the lethal looking things along with a couple paperclips. I opened a hairpin until it was a straight piece of wire and bent it into an L shape. This was called—in the lock-picking biz—a tension wrench.

I then fashioned a pick out of a straightened paperclip. With my tools in my pocket, I paced around the room waiting for Olivia to return.

Five minutes later, she bounded into the room, breathless and gasping for air. "They're all in the dining room. You'd better start with the Bouchers. They're already halfway through their breakfast. The others have just started."

"Right." I squared my shoulder and marched into the hall. When I didn't hear footsteps beside me, I turned and said, "Are you coming?"

Olivia stood in the doorway of our room. "I think not. You're better off without me. I'm afraid you don't know what you're doing, and I don't want to see the results."

I turned back and grabbed her arm. "I need a lookout, and you're it. You have to warn me if someone comes."

Olivia trotted reluctantly toward the Boucher's room. I pulled my tools out of my pocket and bent down to examine the lock.

"What kind of signal should I use?" she asked. "I can't whistle very well when I'm nervous."

I inserted my tension wrench into the bottom of the lock and rotated it as if I were turning a key. Since I haven't tried to break into a room for quite sometime, it took a few tries before I could feel the right tension. Satisfied, I wiggled the pick into the top part of the lock and moved it up and down, listening for a series of clicks.

Next to me, Olivia wrung her hands. "How do you know what you're doing? I just know we're going to be caught."

Suddenly, I felt the tension wrench rotate freely, and I opened the door.

Olivia stared in disbelief. "You did it. I can't believe it, but you did it."

I slipped into the room. "I don't care what signal you use," I told my friend. "Just make sure you warn me. I'll be quick."

I closed the door softly and took three deep breaths to stop my heart from its frantic galloping. And immediately regretted the deep breaths. The room smelled funny—like a combination of mouthwash and smoke. An ashtray full of cigarette butts explained the smoke. The ends were smudged with lipstick, which meant Nicole was the smoker. And married to a cardiologist. And smoking in a hotel room. But I wasn't there to judge. I was there to snoop.

The Bouchers were not neat people. I had no idea how they imagined they could be ready to depart the hotel this morning because stuff was strewn all over the place. On the small desk were three pairs of lace panties, a map of Iceland, a hairdryer, two bags of cookies and a half-eaten power bar.

I stepped over pants and sweaters on the floor and peered into open suitcases. Nothing but the usual clothes you bring on vacation. I was amused, though, to see the good doctor wore tighty whities.

The bathroom yielded nothing interesting. There was a bottle of Advil, a prescription drug I recognized as blood pressure medicine and a circular pill case containing birth control pills. I thought the birth control pills were probably no longer necessary, but I applauded Nicole's optimism. Disappointed, I tiptoed out of the room and closed the door.

Olivia met me in the hall. "Thank heavens! I'm just about peeing my pants. Are you done now?"

"I've been thinking," I said. "Isn't that Cameron's room next door? I think it might be valuable to have a look."

Olivia was puzzled. "Surely you don't believe you'll find anything in there. He was way too broken up over his wife's death. He couldn't have killed her."

"Maybe he's a good actor." I inserted my tension wrench and pick into the lock, and this time the door opened quickly. "Keep a lookout, Olivia. I'll be right back."

In contrast to the Boucher's, Cameron's room was austerely tidy. Someone—I suspected Cameron—had pulled the spread neatly across the bed. Two pieces of luggage stood by the front door, ready to be picked up. One was a simple navy duffle bag and the other a four-wheel brown and tan suitcase with the familiar intertwined *G*s for Gucci. It didn't take a rocket scientist to figure out which suitcase had belonged to Lydia.

The duffle bag was locked, but the zipper on Lydia's wasn't. I hauled the Gucci bag up onto the bed and gingerly opened it. I was sure the police had already inspected it, but I had to have a look. It felt creepy to be going through a dead woman's belongings so I did minimal touching. The police must have examined her clothes, yet everything was neatly folded. Shoes were carefully protected in linen bags. A velvet drawstring bag contained jewelry I'd seen Lydia wear. There were no drugs—not even an aspirin.

I was about to close the bag when I noticed a piece of paper in the zipper compartment on the lid. I almost overlooked it because it resembled some type of flyer. Nevertheless, I pulled it out for a better look. It was a clipping from a Kalispell, Montana, newspaper, dated September 12, 2003:

HIKER DIES IN FALL

Douglas M. Boscoe, 31, died Friday from injuries sustained in a fall while hiking with his wife in Glacier National Park. Mr. Boscoe and his wife, Lara Boscoe, had ventured onto a path that was closed to hikers.

"I told them it was dangerous to hike there," a park ranger told our reporter. "The recent snow had made the paths too slippery. But Mrs. Boscoe insisted they were experienced hikers and would be fine."

"I don't know what happened," she told investigators. "One minute we were admiring the scenery and the next thing I knew he wasn't beside me. He simply disappeared."

After the fall, Mrs. Boscoe was unable to call for help until she reached a ranger station. Her husband's body was found several hours later buried under new snow.

Whoa! Talk about karma. Or foretelling the future. Why would Lydia have this in her suitcase? Very puzzling, but now wasn't a good time to figure it out. I tucked the article into my pocket and slipped out the door. I almost collided with Olivia.

"Well? Did you find anything?"

"Nothing but an old newspaper clipping. I have no idea what it means." I patted my pocket. "But I brought it with me."

Olivia shivered. "Let's get on with it. They'll be starting back soon. I peeked down the stairs and they're assembling in the lobby for the meeting."

I didn't need prodding. I was in the Alessio's room before she finished talking. I headed straight for the bathroom, hoping I'd find a full container of something lethal, which would cause Tangerine to be arrested and put away for a long time. I imagined her body would get fat and lumpy, and her face would sag without all the Botox injections.

Aside from the usual collection of makeup and creams, there was nothing of interest in the bathroom. Disappointed, I went back to the bedroom and got down on my knees to examine the luggage. My heart nearly stopped beating when I heard a loud voice say, "So how was breakfast? Did you try the waffles? If not, you should go back. They're not to be missed."

It was Olivia's voice and that could only mean one thing. The occupants of the room had returned. I frantically looked around for somewhere to hide. Under the bed wouldn't work; there wasn't enough space. The only other place was the closet. I yanked the door open and squeezed as far as I could into a corner. I had chosen Skip's side of the closet. His shirts smelled of perspiration and deodorant, but at the moment I didn't care. I held my breath when I heard a key in the lock, fearing my breathing would give me away.

174 *An Ice Way to Die*

"Why don't you come with me for a drink downstairs." Olivia's voice sounded as scared as I felt.

"Are you completely nuts, lady? It's nine o'clock in the morning." Tangerine was annoyed.

"I was thinking maybe a nice mimosa..."

"Would you please step out of the way and let us into our room?" Her voice was cold and clipped. "Why are you standing there?"

Someone opened the door quickly and banged it shut.

"I'm sick of your mouth. You just don't know when to shut it."

"Don't tell me what to do." Skip's voice was low and menacing. "You'll be sorry if you don't back off."

"And what will happen? Are you going to beat someone else up?" Tangerine laughed. "You'd better curb that temper. I'll bet Emma would love to know you've been arrested for assault. And I'm getting tired of watching you flirt with that woman. What on earth do you see in her? She's not going to invest in your gym, you know. She doesn't have any money. *He* does, and he sure won't give it to her. It didn't work with that obnoxious Cumberland woman, either."

"You should talk about flirting! You're always draped all over that lawyer."

"At least he's nice to me."

In spite of being terrified, I found this very interesting. Which lady did Tangerine mean? Surely not Angela or Emma. Was it Nicole or Ginger? I tried to remember if I'd seen Skip with other women. Nope. He had chatted with Olivia yesterday, but I'm pretty sure he wasn't flirting. Olivia would have said something. And Skip sure didn't sound like the happy-go-lucky guy I knew. Was that demeanor just a "public face?"

I snapped out of my daydreaming when I heard Tangerine say, "I'm so sick of you. I can't wait to get home." Then the sound of a slap, followed by sounds of a scuffle.

What to do, what to do? I didn't want to listen to a physical fight between the two, but I also didn't want to jump out and yell, "Surprise! I was browsing in your closet." I had to think of something fast because the angry voices were drawing nearer to my hiding place.

I was saved by a loud banging on the door and Ginger yelling, "Renee! Skip! Can you please help out here? Olivia seems to have fainted."

I waited until I heard the Alessios run into the hall and converse in low tunes with Olivia, who was apparently sitting up.

"I don't know what came over me," she murmured. "All of a sudden I felt quite faint and suddenly there was nothing. If you could just help me to my room, I'd be ever so thankful."

I had to hand it to my friend. She had just quoted lines from an amateur stage production she'd been in back home. As soon as I heard the door to our room close, I zoomed out of the closet and tore down the stairs to the lobby.

CHAPTER TWENTY

"Ladies and gentlemen, we're on our way to Reykjavik."

Christof sounded perkier today, probably because he would soon be rid of our group.

"After dinner at our hotel, I have arranged a special treat for you. We have heard the Northern Lights are supposed to be spectacular tonight, and we want you to have an opportunity to see them. For those who may be interested, we are going to board the bus around eleven-thirty and drive approximately fifty kilometers outside the city to a cleared field where it is completely dark. Try to sleep before then. It will be a long night. How many of you would like to go?"

I quickly counted hands. Everyone was going. Dirk looked at me questioningly, but I pretended I didn't see him. So far I hadn't had a chance to tell Olivia or him about my room searches. My only regret was I hadn't thought of searching them sooner. We were staying at the Hilton in Reykjavik, and those rooms had sophisticated locks on the doors—ones that would not give in to my amateur attempts at lock busting.

As I studied my fellow passengers, I realized we had all just about reached the end of our social niceness. Tempers flared easily. Petty annoyances that folks tended to ignore in the beginning now sparked arguments. Right now Nicole complained loudly about her husband's use of her face moisturizer. And Ginger and George were having a vigorous fight that I hoped wouldn't result in someone punching someone. It ended when George yelled, "Just be quiet, you stupid bitch!" and Ginger slapped him. Even Emma sat slouched in her seat, her notebook forgotten and a scowl on her face.

"Time to go home," I whispered to Olivia.

"You can say that again, sister. These people look like they're ready to kill each other."

At noon, the bus pulled off the road and stopped in front of a small wooden building. "Hope you all are hungry," Christof said. "This is where we'll eat."

"This doesn't look like much," Olivia said as we walked up the steps. Several others must have thought the same thing because we heard Emma complaining loudly.

"This is not up to our standards, Christof. The brochure clearly says first-class accommodations and food." She pointed her finger at the small structure. "I wouldn't call this first class."

"Please, folks," Christof said as he opened the door. "Do not judge the food until you have tried it. This particular meal is famous in Iceland."

I was willing to try anything since I'd spent breakfast breaking into rooms. The restaurant consisted of one room with tables and chairs on one side and a long table with food on the other. A neon sign above the table advertised Applesin, an orange soft drink, and wine. Christof told us to fill our plates at the buffet and then find a seat.

I watched for an opportunity to speak to Cameron alone, and when I saw him carry his plate to a table, I grabbed a bottle of water and hurried after him.

"Have a drink," I said as I sat down next to him. "This clear, crisp air dries you out."

He accepted my offering without comment and was raising it to his lips as I said, "Could I ask you a few questions? I read somewhere Lydia had a brother who was killed in a hiking accident. That must have been very tough for her." I didn't think I should tell him I found the article while searching his room.

He paused in mid-sip. "Why would you ask me something like that? How do you even know about it?"

"I'm really not prying, but someone Googled Lydia and read an article about her brother."

I had no idea if such an article existed, and I hoped he didn't either. He must have bought my explanation because he said, "Her brother did die, but that was before I knew her. He fell down a mountain while he was hiking. Lydia always suspected his wife had something to do with his death."

Good grief! I hadn't expected this. "Why would Lydia think something like that?"

"She thought Lara, his wife, married her brother for his money. She assumed he was rich because he started a dot com company. Turned out he wasn't. The company went broke. But he had a lot of life insurance."

"Did Lydia stay in contact with her brother's widow?"

"I don't think so. She was born somewhere in Europe, and she went back there after the funeral. No one really cared. She got her insurance money and disappeared. That's all I know."

I nodded in sympathy. "I'm so sorry for your loss. Lydia was far too young to go."

His eyes filled with tears. "Never sick a day in her life and slept like a baby. A bit of high cholesterol perhaps, but otherwise she was against pills and drugs. She firmly believed exercise was the best medicine."

He lowered his eyes and concentrated on his food, and I knew the conversation was over.

The buffet featured hot dogs made mostly with lamb and topped with mustard, ketchup, fried onions and a delightful mixture of mayonnaise and sweet relish.

"Better to order two right away," Christof told us. "You will want two. I promise."

He was right. They tasted terrific and surpassed any hot dog I'd ever eaten. Even Emma stopped muttering when she tried the delicious concoction. I gobbled down two of these wonderful creations and an orange drink far too quickly. My pants felt like they were going to burst at my waist, so before this could happen I stepped outside to discreetly open the top button. Just as I took a deep breath and prepared to let it all hang out, a voice stopped me.

"I've been trying to talk to you, Julia. You always seem to be so busy."

The voice was petulant, and it belonged to Angela. I hurriedly zipped up and turned to face her.

"I didn't realize you were trying to speak to me. What's up?"

"Many things. Have you been paying attention to what the hidden people are saying?"

Not this again! I'd almost forgotten about trolls and elves. "I haven't heard them speak lately. Have you?"

I couldn't help staring at Angela. She wore a long green skirt, a purple striped jacket, a pair of very bizarre red, orange and yellow sneakers and the ever-present ruana. On her head was a pink turban covered in sparkling sequins.

"That's quite a hat, Angela. Where did you get it? Did you bring it from home?"

She patted her head. "Of course not, silly. Gudrun gave it to me. She said she wanted to always be able to find me."

"That was very nice of her. Has she been with us on the whole trip?"

"Certainly. Where did you think she would go?" She looked at me slyly. "Have you seen her yet?"

This surprised me. "Should I have seen her? Is she on the bus with us?"

"I don't think so."

"What does that mean? Is she or isn't she?"

Angela pulled a large handkerchief of dubious cleanliness out of her bag and swished it across her nose. "She might be on the bus. She might be hidden under a seat or something because, you know, hidden people know how to hide."

This was like talking to a squirrel. "But you haven't actually seen Gudrun on the bus. Right?"

"Not actually, but she says she's always with us." She lowered her voice as if she were afraid of being overheard. "I need to talk to you about her."

My ears perked up. Maybe we were finally going to get somewhere. "Is there something wrong with Gudrun?"

Angela looked upset. "The thing is, she seems to know everything that's happening. For instance, she knew I had herring for breakfast."

"We all knew that, Angela. We could smell the onions."

"But she said she didn't like me talking to Renee. She told me to sit by myself at the next meal. I'd been sitting with Renee, but how could she know that? She wasn't in the dining room."

Ah, but she must have been, but I didn't share that with Angela. "This is important. Can you remember who else from our group was having breakfast?"

"Everyone but you and Olivia. Dirk and the Bouchers came in just as I was leaving." She shivered. "I used to like Gudrun a lot, but lately I've been a little afraid of her. She also has friends who aren't hidden people. That's not good."

"How do you know that? And what kind of people are we talking about?"

"Two men. And I know they're not *huldufólk* because hidden people don't drink spirits."

"Spirits? What are spirits?" I didn't know if she meant wispy apparitions that were somehow potable or the distilled kind that tasted good and came in a bottle.

"Alcohol. I heard the men say they would meet Gudrun at a bar for a drink. Hidden people would never do that."

Angela sounded almost sane today so I thought I'd try a question. "I need to ask you something I've been wondering about. Why are you so afraid of Dirk? He's really a very nice man." I supposed to some people this was probably true.

Her face immediately closed. "I can't talk about him."

"Why not? Help me out here because I really don't understand."

Her fingers fumbled nervously with the fringe on her ruana. "Don't ask me, Julia."

"Please tell me," I said softly. "You don't have to be afraid. Whatever it is, I'm sure we can sort it out."

"Well, we can't. You want to know why? We can't because he's dead. He can't be here."

Okay, then. Maybe she wasn't as sane as I thought.

I took a deep breath and said, "He's not dead. What would give you that idea? I'm not sure what you mean."

But Angela wasn't listening. She had her hands over her ears and was shaking her head vigorously back and forth. There was no point in trying to talk to her anymore. And the rest of our group had finished lunch and were outside ready to leave.

Olivia caught up with me at the bus. "I saw you chatting with our loony friend. Did she have anything interesting to say?"

"I think the elusive Gudrun is on the bus," I whispered. "I'll tell you later."

I sat down in my seat and promptly went to sleep, which was probably due to the tasty, calorie-filled hot dogs I'd just consumed. And the two excellent beers I forgot to mention.

"Finally back in civilization. I love this hotel." Tangerine pulled the cap off her head and shook out her blond hair. "I've had enough bus-riding for a while. It seemed to take forever to get here. All this sitting is flattening my ass."

Several men standing nearby checked to see if this was true.

Our little group filed into the lobby of the Hilton Reykjavik Nordica and, since our rooms weren't available yet, flopped down on the couches and chairs.

"Those who wish to see the Northern Lights please be at the front door at ten thirty tonight," Christof reminded us. "Until then, enjoy your day in Reykjavik."

"Who's for some shopping?" Tangerine asked. "We have to wait until our rooms are ready, so we might as well see what's in the stores. Anyone want to go?"

Olivia, Nicole, Ginger, Tangerine and I immediately stood up and headed to the door. As we passed the reception desk, a concierge, who'd been helping a guest, looked up and glanced at our group. The expression on his face turned from polite helpfulness to real pleasure. He smiled broadly and called, "Astrid! Hey! How are you doing? It's great to see you again!"

We swiveled our heads, searching for the person in question, and seeing no one we continued across the lobby. The concierge came around the desk and walked towards us.

"Are you staying with us, Astrid? Maybe we can meet for a drink later."

We stopped walking because he was obviously talking to us. "Do you know this guy?" I asked in a whisper. The others shook their heads. I gave him a friendly smile and shrugged my shoulders, indicating there was no Astrid here. His face turned bright red as he hastily mumbled an apology and backed away.

"That was odd," I said once we were outside. "He obviously thought he recognized one of us."

Ginger pulled sunglasses out of her bag and wiped them on a tissue. "I get that all the time. I must have a very generic face because people are always telling me I look like someone else."

We nodded. This had happened to us, too. Well, most of us. Tangerine patted her hair and said, "Not me. No one ever mistakes me for someone else. I'm one of a kind, baby."

Of course you are, buttercup.

CHAPTER TWENTY-ONE

I figured some of us would opt for sleep rather than a bus trip to see the Northern Lights, but we were all there. As we took our seats, Christof stood in the front with the mic in his hand.

"This should be a real treat, which I hope you all will enjoy. We are going to drive about an hour from the city to a flat spot high on a hill and away from all the lights. Since we cannot predict when or even if they will appear, we will have time for conversation or sleep. Or perhaps a snack if any of you brought food." He smiled. "Do not worry. If you fall asleep, we will wake you for the show. In any event, enjoy this amazing and mystical spectacle."

"This had better be worth it." Olivia stretched out her legs and leaned back against the seat. "I think I'd rather be sleeping."

She and I sat by ourselves near the rear of the bus. Christof had lowered the lights, making reading difficult. I waited until I thought the others might be dozing and then said, "Didn't you find it odd the concierge thought he recognized one of us?"

She yawned. "Not really. He probably sees so many people, he just got confused."

"But if my theory is right—that Lydia's killer is one of us—maybe he recognized her. It just seems strange he'd look so confident when he called Astrid," I persisted.

"You say 'he recognized *her*.' Are you convinced we're looking for a woman?"

I considered this. "I guess so. Probably because of all that stuff about Gudrun and elves. Although Serge might have had a motive to kill Lydia. And maybe Nathan would kill to protect Emma, but I really can't see that. Skip and George don't seem to have motives. I don't think Cameron killed his wife."

"You seem to have left out one," Olivia said. "What about Dirk?"

"Honestly, Olivia, he's a lawyer. I think he'd be above committing a crime like that."

"My, my," she said. "Are we just a little bit blind about him? Anyway, I think your imagination is working overtime. No one from our group has ever been in Iceland before this trip, so the concierge couldn't have recognized one of us."

"People lie, Olivia. One of them could be lying. It makes sense to think the killer has been here before. Angela said Gudrun had taught her an Icelandic phrase. And someone with knowledge of the area knew how to get Angela up on the rocks in Vik. Know what I think? I'm convinced the elusive Gudrun is one of us."

I could feel Olivia staring at me in the darkness. "You should probably keep your voice down," she whispered. "But tell me, how exactly would that work? The people in our group are always with us."

"Are they? We go to the bathroom, or buy food and souvenirs in shops or simply wander around enjoying the sights. No one keeps track of us all the time."

"Let's suppose you're right," Olivia said. "This would mean whoever it is has to change clothes very quickly. How would that work?"

"Piece of cake," I told her. "We're all carrying tote bags, and they're certainly roomy enough to hold garments. Someone disappears for a few minutes, quickly plays the role of Gudrun and is back before anyone becomes suspicious. I'm thinking of the night

Dirk and I saw Angela walking with someone. That person could easily have pulled off a coat or jacket, stuffed it in a bag and headed back to the hotel."

"This is all very interesting," Olivia said, "but if Gudrun is someone in our group, why doesn't Angela recognize her?"

I sighed. "That's a good question. I don't know."

Suddenly the mic came on and Christof said, "Look out the window, folks. It is beginning."

Sure enough, we saw a faint green glow in the dark. As we watched, it grew bigger and brighter until it resembled a gauzy curtain billowing in the sky.

I felt a tap on my shoulder. Emma stood in front of us holding a paper plate of food. "We had some sweet things to share, but this is all we have left—some crackers and cheese and these terribly fattening chocolate balls. Why are you two way back here? There are plenty of seats near the front."

"Thank you, Emma." To prevent further conversation, Olivia put the plate on the seat between us, folded her arms across her stomach and closed her eyes.

As soon as Emma was gone, Olivia said, "Do you want these? I'm not hungry."

I eyed the chocolate goodies. They looked decadent and probably contained a million calories, but we were on vacation, and everyone knew calories didn't count on vacation.

"I'll take those," I told her. "I need the sugar to keep up my energy." I bit into one, and was slightly disappointed at the taste. It was almost too sweet, if that was possible. The chocolate fudge icing was tasty enough, but the dough itself was a bit off. I decided whoever baked these had used artificial sweetener. Nevertheless, I ate half of it and wrapped the rest in a napkin to be disposed of later.

Both of us stopped talking and watched the astounding sight. Shimmering waves of green filled the sky. It was eerie and beautiful all at once, and I'd never seen anything like it. I was mesmerized, so when I suddenly fell forward and clonked my head on the seat in front of me, Olivia was understandably surprised.

I woke up to find myself lying on the backseat Lydia had recently vacated, and Nicole, Ginger and Emma were hovering over me fanning my face. I had a horrible taste in my mouth and my tongue felt like it had licked something nasty.

"What happened? How did I get back here? And please stop waving your hands in my face."

Olivia was actually wringing her hands. "You all of a sudden conked out. I was really scared. When I couldn't wake you up, I asked Dirk to bring you back here so you could lie down. Emma wanted to give you one of her potions, but I didn't think that was a good idea."

It certainly was not. And I didn't want to discuss anything, especially with Emma hanging over me and Angela chanting something about trolls putting a spell on me. I wanted to go back to the hotel, get into bed and wait for it to be time to go home. Because I was pretty sure I hadn't fallen asleep on my own. I had been wide awake and enjoying the astounding Northern Lights and certainly not intending to doze off. I was sure I'd been drugged.

CHAPTER TWENTY-TWO

I felt awful. My head hurt and my stomach wasn't willing to accept anything—not even the Pepto-Bismol Olivia was urging me to swallow. She fluttered around me, smoothing my pillow and straightening the sheets.

"I don't understand why I have to be in bed."

"Dirk wants to make sure whatever knocked you out is gone. Your face still looks like a pot of paste."

I propped myself up on one elbow. "Since when is he a doctor? And what do you mean whatever knocked me out? You know perfectly well what it was. Someone tried to kill me with that ketamine stuff."

I got out of bed and wobbled toward my clothes on the chair. "I'm not sticking around here to give whoever is doing this another chance. I'm going home. Right now."

Olivia looked upset. "Please don't leave me here by myself. We're going home the day after tomorrow. I'm going to call Dirk. He'll make sure nothing happens."

Suddenly the room started spinning, and I sat down on the edge of the bed.

"See! You're not okay. Let me get Dirk."

"I don't know what you think he can do. I just want to get out of here."

But Olivia wasn't listening. She was on the phone, motioning to me to be quiet. "He'll be here in a minute," she said as she hung up. "Please stop worrying. You'll be safe."

Bah! That's probably what they told Marie Antoinette as she strolled through the Tuileries Garden.

Even in my weakened, nauseated state, I wondered what I looked like. I should comb my hair or at least brush my teeth. My mouth felt like a dirty, smelly critter had marched through it. Dirk knocked on the door before I had a chance to overhaul myself.

Once in the room, he eyed me critically. "I've seen you looking better."

"Very funny." I kept my hand over my mouth since I was pretty sure my breath wasn't minty fresh.

"So..." he began.

"So someone tried to kill me with that stuff. I'm pretty sure it was in something I ate on the bus."

"But we all ate," Olivia interjected. "Well, I didn't, but I'll bet the rest did. And no one else conked out in the middle of the festivities."

I stood up, and this time my legs worked. "All I know is someone made sure I got the deadly food. It must have been in the chocolate ball. That's all I ate. And Emma gave it to us."

"But how could the person be sure Julia would eat the chocolate?"

Olivia patted her flat stomach. "Look at me. Do I look like I'd eat gooey chocolate? This person had to know Julia would gobble it up."

"Excuse me. I did not gobble it up. It didn't taste quite right, so I wrapped half of it in a napkin and stuck it in the pocket on my backpack. I intended to throw it away later."

Dirk was across the room and upending my backpack before I could stop him. He opened the zipper and pulled out a pair of socks, a bunch of menus from our lunchroom and a BEGINNING CHINESE book I kept meaning to study.

"Where in this mess would I find the food?"

I snatched the backpack out of his hand and reached into the side pocket where I had crammed the rest of the chocolate ball. But it was empty.

"I don't understand," I said. "I'm positive I put it in here." A careful inspection of the rest of the bag revealed nothing.

"Did anyone touch this?" Dirk asked.

"You're asking me? I wasn't watching."

Dirk looked at Olivia. "Did you see anything?"

My friend shook her head. "Everyone was so worried about Julia. They were all trying to help her. Anyone could have picked it up."

"But someone had to know the chocolate ball was in the backpack. Someone watched me hide it."

Olivia shuddered. "I'm so glad we're going home soon."

I grabbed my clothes and went into the bathroom to dress. As I pulled on my pants, I noticed the newspaper clipping I had purloined from Lydia's suitcase was still in my pocket.

"Here," I said when I returned to the bedroom. "Have a look at this. I found it in Lydia's suitcase. I have no idea what it means or if it has anything to do with her death."

Dirk glanced at it briefly and handed it back to me. "I'll look at it later. Right now I want you to promise me you'll stay in this room. We're lucky this is a free day with nothing scheduled. If you want to go out, call me. I'll be back soon."

His face looked serious as he strode to the door. And I had no intention of staying in the room. I was feeling steadier on my feet and the thought of a bit of exercise and fresh air appealed to me. I even felt a little hungry. As soon as Olivia left, saying she was going shopping with Nicole, I made my move.

Armed with a guidebook, I exited the hotel and strolled towards Laugavegur, a shopping area in Reykjavik. There were wonderful shops there—gift shops, book shops, kitchen shops, ice cream shops. Many of the stores were painted in happy colors. For instance, there was a red house with a blue roof and yellow window frames. Next to it was a cobalt blue building and next to that a house painted pink on one side and mustard yellow on the other. Most of the restaurants and cafés had tables and chairs on the sidewalk.

Suddenly the idea of a hot dog slathered in onions and sauce made me drool. I walked quickly past a shop selling ladies underwear and nightgowns. Very pretty stuff. I thought about my sensible cotton panties and my "Sleeps with the Dog" nightshirt and wondered if I should buy something sexy. But why? My dog didn't care.

Up ahead I saw a sign for an herbal medicine shop. My guidebook said the owner followed an old Icelandic tradition of making all kinds of ointments and oils. And much to my astonishment, an unmistakable figure stood in the doorway. Angela, dressed in her ever-present ruana, appeared to be deep in conversation with a smaller person. I would have bet everything she was talking to Gudrun.

What to do? This time I was smart enough not to run wildly toward them yelling at the top of my lungs. Instead, I ducked into a small shop and watched.

Angela seemed agitated. She shook her head repeatedly as she listened. I couldn't identify her companion. The person wasn't tall and wore a long raincoat, which seemed out of place in this weather. It was impossible to determine if it was a man or a woman, but from the way he/she moved, I decided it had to be a woman.

I was pretending to peruse a copy of *The Reyjavik Grapevine* when suddenly Angela turned and stalked off. Her friend waited a few minutes and much to my delight, walked down Laugavegur in the direction of the hotel. I allowed her to get several yards ahead of me before I turned to follow. She walked quickly and carried a large shopping bag. Twice I had to duck behind parked cars to prevent being noticed when the person turned around.

I had to hurry when she turned into the entrance of a shop. At least I thought it was a shop, but as I approached, I saw it was a café with a chalkboard outside advertising different kinds of coffee. I opened the door and looked around. The interior was small and cozy with no more than six round tables. The place smelled delicious. At the far end was a counter with small sandwiches and pastries, which reminded me of our lunchroom in Wake Forest.

I quickly scanned the room, looking for the person I'd followed, but she was nowhere. Could I have been mistaken? Did she perhaps turn into the shop next door? I turned to leave and almost jumped out of my socks when a voice called, "Yoo hoo, Julia! Over here!"

Olivia sat at a table in the corner, along with Emma and Nicole. "Come join us. I went back to the hotel to check on you and was worried when you weren't in the room." She gave me a stern look. "Weren't you supposed to stay there?"

I wanted to say Dirk wasn't going to tell me what to do, but that would have necessitated an explanation to the other ladies, so I ignored her.

"I'm looking for someone who just came in here. At least I think she did."

Olivia raised her eyebrows. "Who would that be?"

"It doesn't matter. I don't see her here."

"Well, as you can see, the place isn't crowded." She consulted her watch. "Ginger is supposed to meet us here in a minute."

At the mention of her name, Ginger entered the café, and I had to admit she looked good. Her red hair floated in a cloud around her head. She wore a soft yellow sweater and white skirt with a diagonal splash of yellow. And five-inch heel sandals. She sure wasn't dressed for doughnuts with the girls.

"I went out to lunch with George," she said. "We went to another hotel that was supposed to have a fancy restaurant, so I dressed up a bit."

Olivia pulled out a chair for me, all the time raving about the shopping opportunities. "Julia, you have to see the store we found. It has the most gorgeous clothes and accessories. I bought the most beautiful handbag. It cost a fortune, but I can take it everywhere."

"Where, exactly, would everywhere be? We live in the country. Our biggest social event is a street party in Wake Forest. We're jeans people."

Olivia scowled at me. "I'm sure I have other gracious social activities to attend. Ones that you don't know about."

"Really?" I wanted to challenge her, but this wasn't the time or the place and if she actually did have other social opportunities, well, good for her. I had something else on my mind.

"Did you see a person come in here? I think whoever it was has dark hair and was wearing a long trench coat with a hood." I suddenly felt a bit silly. "I think it might have been this Gudrun person Angela talks about."

"Seeing hidden people now, Julia?" Ginger asked with a smile.

"I've met her, you know," Emma said. "I'd be able to identify her." She looked around the small café. "She's not here."

Olivia rolled her eyes. "Thank you, Emma." She turned to me. "Why did you think she'd be here?"

"It's a bit of a long story, but I thought I saw her come in this door, but I must have been wrong. The shops are so close together, she must have entered one of the others. Emma, maybe you could come with me to the next store. If she's taken off her coat, you'll be able to recognize her."

Emma squirmed in her seat. "I…ah, may not be able to definitively identify her. I mean, I certainly have seen her, but she and I haven't actually conversed."

I narrowed my eyes. "What does that mean you haven't 'actually conversed?' You mean you've never met her?"

"Well, not *per se*. I've certainly seen her but we've never been formally introduced."

Olivia and I exchanged glances. "Where have you seen her? Have you seen her face?"

Emma pushed back from the table and clutched her bag to her chest. "I don't have to stay here and be interrogated, Julia Greene. Go find her yourself. I'm not going to help you."

Swell. "How about you two?" I said to Ginger and Nicole. "I'm assuming you've all heard Angela talk about her friend, Gudrun. Have either of you seen her?"

Both ladies shook their heads. "I've heard Angela talk about her," Ginger said, "but I never pay much attention to her. She seems to be a pretty disturbed person. I'm surprised she's still with us."

Nicole nodded. "I know Lark Tours has tried to contact her family but hasn't had any luck. Christof asked my husband if there was anything he could do. I think he wanted him to prescribe medication, but he can't do that."

"Of course not. He would have to examine Angela before giving her any drugs," Olivia said

Nicole looked down at her hands. "It isn't that. He isn't allowed to prescribe anything anymore. He had some sort of psychotic episode some years ago and the AMC decided it would be better if he didn't practice medicine anymore. He's fine now, of course. He had therapy and medication." She shook her head. "It was all very unfortunate and stemmed from an incident that happened long ago."

"I'm sorry," Olivia said. "I certainly wasn't trying to be nosy."

The atmosphere was decidedly morose, so to lighten the mood I ordered decadent chocolate cakes and coffee for everyone. Forty minutes later, I waddled out of the café vowing not to eat again until I was back home in Wake Forest.

I left the café extremely puzzled. I'd been so sure the figure I was following had come in here. As I walked slowly towards the hotel, I realized several buildings were similar to the café. For instance, a small house a short distance away had the same façade with the same green awning over the entrance. This house was blue and yellow and could have used some sprucing up. Weeds choked the path to the steps, which was uncharacteristic for this well-kept neighborhood.

I couldn't determine if it was a business or a private residence. There were large black and white photos on easels in the window, so I deduced it might be a photography studio. But the display certainly wasn't designed to attract customers. The windows were dirty and the whole place looked uncared for.

Nevertheless, I had to find Gudrun. If she wasn't here, I'd give up and go back to the hotel. I walked up the steps and tried the door. To my surprise, it opened. I took a tentative step onto the old wood floor, wincing as it creaked under my feet. It took me a few minutes to get my bearings. I called hello, not loud enough to attract anyone in the back of the house but enough to alert anyone ready to jump out at me. When there was no answer, I decided to look around.

To the left was what I supposed was the living room, but there was no furniture—only the easels and several large pictures mounted on cardboard and stacked against the wall. The room across the hall contained a wooden table and nothing else. The table was piled with papers and magazines—and the bag I'd seen the elusive Gudrun carrying. Even though I was terrified I'd be caught, I couldn't resist peeking.

Inside was the long raincoat I'd seen Gudrun wearing and a pair of black walking shoes. And a pink headband with sequins. My discovery made my heart beat so fast I was afraid I was going to pass out. I knew who owned that headband! By damn, I had solved the case. I was picturing the guilty person in an orange jumpsuit when a voice from somewhere in the back called, "Astrid, is that you?"

Oh boy! I debated what to do. I could say I came to ask about photos, but my hand was in the cookie jar, so to speak. I put the headband in my pocket as footsteps on the floor indicated someone was about to discover me.

He was tall and blond and fit. What was it with these Icelanders? They all looked so healthy. But I wasn't here to assess this man's fitness level. I just wanted to get out.

"I'm sorry to have burst in like this. I'm looking for a friend and thought I saw her come in here. I was obviously mistaken." When he didn't answer, I said, "Do you speak English?"

He smiled. "As a matter of fact I do. How can I help you?"

He sounded sincere, which made me relax a little.

"I'm looking for a friend named Gudrun. I saw her earlier in town but didn't have a chance to talk to her."

"I see."

I tend to babble in awkward situations, and I began to babble now. "I just wanted to ask her a few questions, but I can see you're busy, and if she's not here, I won't take anymore of your time."

"Please come with me. I will get her."

He indicated the long hall and pointed to what I assumed was the kitchen at the end of it. "You will wait in there while I tell her you are here."

"That's not necessary." Now I was really scared. There was no way I wanted to go anywhere with this man. "I can come back later."

"Please." He stepped aside and motioned for me to go first. "We will wait in there together."

"I really can't do this," I protested. "My friends will be worried when I don't get back to the hotel."

He didn't appear to be listening. I had no choice but to do as I was told. Once in the kitchen, he pulled out a chair at a table and said. "Sit. I can see you are uncomfortable. Would you care for something to drink?"

I shook my head. "All I want to do is go to the hotel—and then back to North Carolina and my home that I never intend to leave again." And I certainly didn't want anything to drink. The drink would probably have hemlock or something in it.

From somewhere beyond the kitchen a phone rang. The man's hands flew to his pocket, obviously looking for his cell.

"Please stay seated," he said as he rose from the chair. "I will be back in a minute and we can talk about this Gudrun."

My mother didn't raise a dummy. As soon as he was gone, I got up, raced down the hall and out the front door. I ran all the way to the hotel, terrified someone would grab me around the neck and haul me back to the house. I couldn't wait to get back to the hotel and find Dirk because I knew who Gudrun was. It was Tangerine, my favorite person in the whole world.

CHAPTER TWENTY-THREE

I burst into the lobby as if my pants were on fire. I was wheezing so hard my chest hurt every time I took a breath, which probably indicated some kind of heart disease, but at the moment I didn't care. I saw Dirk sitting at a table with Olivia and the Bouchers. I careened up to them, clamped my hand onto Dirk's arm and said, "I would like to speak to you." Realizing I resembled some kind of wild person, I pushed my hair, which now hung in wet clumps, out of my face and tried a smile. "How are you doin?" I asked the group.

They all sprang to their feet. "Are you having a medical emergency?" Serge asked, his face full of concern. "Come over here and sit down." He already had his fingers on the pulse in my wrist.

I shook my head, spraying everyone with sweat. "I'm good. Just went for a little jog. Dirk, can I speak to you or not?"

"Of course. Why don't we go outside so you can cool off a bit. You went jogging, you say?"

He was treating me like a difficult child, but I didn't have time to berate him. We went to the door with Olivia following.

"I'm coming, too. You look like you've gone mad."

We walked—with me in the middle and Dirk and Olivia on either side—until my breathing sounded more regular and the searing pain in my chest subsided. When we were far enough away from curious eyes at the hotel, we sat down on a bench.

"I take it something's wrong," Dirk said.

"I've solved the case," I said smugly.

"Go ahead," Dirk said. "I'm very curious to hear what you have to say."

I was surprised at their reaction. I guess I expected hoots and hollers and cries of "By Jove, well done!"

"Why aren't you more elated? I know who Gudrun is."

"Julia, you got excited when the hotel in Selfoss served grapefruit juice," he reminded me. "We need to hear what you've found before we do the happy dance."

So I told them about seeing Angela and Gudrun, and visiting the house, and talking to the man. And then I produced my ace. I pulled the headband out of my pocket and waved it in the air.

"See this? I found it in the backpack Gudrun was carrying. Do you know who owns this? The lovely Tangerine. She was wearing it the night we went out on the boat. You must remember, Dirk. She was very attentive to you that evening."

Dirk looked confused. "Who?"

I forgot Olivia and I hadn't shared her real name with him. "Renee, of course. It's a long story and I'll fill you in later. And what does it matter what we call her? This is the proof we needed."

Instead of clapping her hands in approval, Olivia bit her lip. "Oh my goodness, Julia. I hate to burst your bubble but..." She reached into her bag and pulled out an identical headband. "We all have them. Well, maybe not Angela. We bought them the first day at a little shop not far from here. We thought they were so cute. Don't you have one?"

Talk about being doused with cold water! I didn't have a headband because I hadn't gone shopping with them. I didn't like shopping under the best of circumstances but it was definitely not my idea of fun right after a nine-hour flight. Deflated, I dropped the headband back in my pocket.

"Cheer up," Dirk said. "This proves Gudrun is one of the group. I know we suspected it, but this proves it."

"Why does it prove it?" I asked. "Maybe a complete stranger walked into that shop and bought the same headband. Plenty of tourists visited that store."

"That would be too much of a coincidence. I think we're getting a pretty good picture of this Gudrun. Think of all the incidents with Angela being in unlikely situations as a result of contact with her. I think this person has a good knowledge of Iceland. She may even speak the language."

"You're right," I said. "Remember when Angela said she learned an Icelandic phrase from Gudrun?"

"And remember when the concierge at the hotel called out the name Astrid?" Olivia said. "The concierge must have recognized one of us as someone he knew as Astrid. Maybe Astrid is Gudrun's real name, and the name she uses on the tour is an alias."

"Astrid!" I almost screamed. "The man at the house thought I was Astrid at first. I'd forgotten all about the concierge at the hotel. Plus, this man obviously has some connection to Gudrun. But what?"

"I always wondered how Angela managed to get up on the rocks or in a tree," Dirk said. "We know she couldn't do those things by herself. The elusive Gudrun had to have help. It must have been this man."

"So we can conclude Gudrun has been in Iceland before. Maybe she's even lived here. She speaks the language and has friends in Reykjavik. And she's also on our tour."

Hearing Dirk say this gave me chills. "But what possible motive could this person have for killing Lydia or wanting me out of the way?"

Dirk stood up and pulled me to my feet. "I don't know. I think we have all the clues. We just have to figure it out."

CHAPTER TWENTY-FOUR

It may be Iceland's premier tourist attraction, but from the minute I walked in the door, I was pretty sure I wasn't going to like the Blue Lagoon. First of all, there were a lot of rules, which I discovered after reading the brochure as we waited in line to check in. There was one rule I found particularly disturbing—guests were required to shower naked before donning bathing suits and entering the water. The only person who'd ever shared a shower with me was my husband, and I had no intention of starting communal bathing now.

And secondly, there were a lot of people—even though it was fairly late in the day. While the group in front of us laughed and chatted in a foreign language, I looked around for a way to escape. Olivia must have had the same thought because she poked me in the ribs and said, "We're stuck here. The bus is gone. Christof said he was taking it to get gas."

"I sincerely do not want to do this," I said. "They have a gift shop. Maybe we can wait there."

But we'd already reached the front of the line. A woman handed me a wrist bracelet and explained how to use it. "Find an empty locker. This is your key. Create a code of your own and a password and simply hold the wristband over the lock and your belongings will be secure. Do not lose this wristband," she warned. "If you do, it will cost you ISK 5000 for a replacement."

I fumbled with the clasp as we walked down the long hall to the dressing room. Once inside, Olivia,

Emma, Nicole, Angela, Ginger, Tangerine and I located seven lockers together and stood around self-consciously wondering what to do next. It was one thing to travel together and eat meals together. It was something completely different to undress together.

The ladies across from us had no such problem. They stripped their clothes off, stuck them in the lockers and then chatted as if they were having a morning *kaffee klatch*. There was an overwhelming plethora of naked breasts and butts bouncing around the room as if we were in the middle of some kind of mid-summer frolic. I noticed one of their bags was decorated with the Swedish flag. Ah, the free spirits of the Nordic people. I was sure they thought we Americans were positively Victorian, which I guess we were because we were still standing there fully dressed and with our mouths open.

"I really don't care for this," Nicole said. "I had no idea it would be—well—so public."

Even Tangerine seemed subdued. And I felt sorry for Angela. She sat on the bench with her bag in her lap and a defiant look on her face. "The hidden people don't want me to do this. There are elves living in the lagoon."

Ginger sat down next to her. "I think the hidden people want to show you where they live. Don't you want to see?"

It was as if she was speaking to a child, but I was grateful for her concern. When Angela nodded in agreement and began to shed her clothes, I turned away.

A woman attendant clapped her hands and said, "Let us hurry, ladies. Others are waiting to experience the lagoon. Take off all your clothes and step into the shower."

Ginger faced her locker as she discreetly undressed and wrapped a towel around her. When Tangerine peeled off her clothes, I tried not to look, but it was impossible to miss her surgically enhanced boobs. They were quite perky.

"Come on, Olivia. I guess we have to get this over with," I said, but Olivia was already stepping out of her pants.

"It's not so bad once you do it," she said. "Besides, who's looking? We're all females here. And you'd better tighten that wristband. You don't want to have to pay to replace it."

So I undressed, threw my clothes in the locker, swiped the bracelet over the lock and wrapped the towel around me. I was planning to avoid the shower by somehow hurrying past it, but the attendant was directing traffic.

"Use soap, ladies," she intoned. "We want to keep our water clean."

I ditched the towel, ducked under the shower, retrieved my towel and headed back to the dressing room to grab my bathing suit. Olivia followed me. She had the towel wrapped around her head instead of her body.

Once safely enveloped in terrycloth, I said, "Do you realize the towel is around your head? I only mention this because I thought the rest of you might be chilly."

"Actually, I'm feeling quite normal like this. Quite free."

"You're quite nuts. Let's get this over with."

Olivia and I put on our bathing suits and headed to the lagoon.

My first impression of the geothermal spa was that it was, indeed, blue. And the water was hot. Steam rose from the surface, drifting over the lava rocks surrounding it and making the whole place resemble an eerie lunar landscape. My first tentative step into the lagoon told me I wouldn't be staying long. It was too warm. And due to the high sulfur content in the water, I caught whiffs of a smell I hoped wouldn't linger on my body.

I tried to locate the rest of our group. Angela was in the water and apparently safe from hidden people. Ginger and George floated next to her. Skip was surrounded by a group of the ladies from Sweden. When I saw him hoist one up and put her on his shoulders, I looked around for Tangerine, but she was nowhere in sight.

"You have to try the silica," Olivia exclaimed as she smeared white stuff all over her face. "This is supposed to give you a special glow."

"You go ahead and glow," I said as I waded further into the water. I was not feeling my usual happy self. Yesterday's meeting with the man in the house had scared me more than I wanted to admit. I couldn't wait to go home.

"Why's your brow furrowed like that?"

I didn't even notice Dirk until he was standing next to me. I must have been in exceedingly bad shape because he was a hard man not to see—especially in swimming trunks. He looked terrific. Suddenly I was very aware I was wearing an old bathing suit that didn't fit as well as it used to, but when I was packing for the trip back home in Wake Forest, I hadn't imagined meeting a man.

"People look better with their clothes on, don't they?" I said hoping to direct his attention away from me.

"You don't. I like the way you look."

"I'll bet you say that to all the girls." Good grief! I was simpering.

He smiled at me with his eyes. "Actually, I haven't said that to anyone for a long time."

I didn't know how to answer that. I was acutely aware that he and I were standing in a giant bathtub without much on.

"Julia, I know I haven't said anything about our—well—you know, but that doesn't mean I haven't thought about it. With everything going on, there hasn't been a private second to talk about it."

I wanted to dispute that and tell him there certainly had been. I thought about all the times I'd lurked in the shadows waiting for him to say something, but for once, I kept my mouth shut. This was fortunate because his next words made me feel great.

"I just want you to know I don't do that sort of thing. Ever. And I don't think you do either."

"Nope," I said, not trusting my voice. "I think you could say that was my first one-night stand."

He winced. "You make it sound kind of sleazy. You don't feel that way, do you?"

I didn't want to tell him how I felt. It was enough to know he was talking to me now.

"I felt something special between us. I thought maybe you did, too," he said.

"Yes, well… I probably wouldn't have done that if I hadn't."

He put his arm around my shoulder and pulled me close. "Good. It was wonderful, you know."

So was this it? He tells me we had a special connection and it was wonderful, and then he goes on with this life? I wished Olivia was there to tell me to stop acting like an idiot. It was what it was. Period. We were all parting ways soon, and we'd never see each other again.

He started to say more, but Angela hurried up to us, obviously distressed. And she looked like she'd arisen from the bottom of the lagoon. She had smeared the white silica not only on her face, but all over her body, including her bathing suit and hair.

"Angela, didn't you read the sign? You're not supposed to get the water or that stuff in your hair. You are going to have a tough time getting it off."

She waved away my concerns. "I don't care about that. I want to leave here because some people aren't being nice to me."

I glanced at Dirk. "Jump in anytime."

"What's wrong?" Dirk asked. "Are you having trouble with someone in our group?"

She scraped a thick blob off her face and flicked it into the water. "I was talking to Ginger and George when Renee came up behind me and splashed me. I splashed her back, but some of the water got on Ginger and she shrieked like I'd hit her or something. 'Get away from me, you idiot! Don't get my hair wet.' I didn't mean to do it."

"Of course you didn't," Dirk said soothingly. "Ginger probably saw the sign that said the water will dry out your hair." He eyed the mess on top of her head. "I think that's why Julia is concerned about you."

"I don't like these people, and the *huldufólk* don't, either. Maybe one of them can turn Ginger into a troll wife."

Oh boy! It really was time to go home. "Walk with me, Angela. The nice warm water will make you feel better." As Dirk took Angela's arm and led her away, he turned and winked at me. Since Angela was terrified of him, I was amazed she went willingly, until I heard her say, "You're dead, you know. I think you must be invisible."

I'd had enough of the Blue Lagoon. The smell of sulfur and the hot water were making me feel sick. Maybe some people enjoyed this, but I sure didn't. I scanned the bobbing heads for Olivia and, not seeing her, decided to leave without her. Since she knew this wasn't my idea of fun, she'd correctly assume I'd left.

I knew the rules required a nude shower also after leaving the spa, but this time the attendant wasn't there, and I hurried to the dressing room without anyone stopping me. In fact, there was only one other lady in the room and she was busy drying her hair.

Relieved, I secured the towel around my middle and looked for my locker. I couldn't quite remember the number, but since all our lockers were together, and I knew the general location, it would simply be a matter of trial and error until I found the correct one.

At first, when I didn't feel my wristband on my left arm, I thought I'd put it on the right one. My stomach lurched when it wasn't there either. I couldn't remember when I'd last seen it, but I hadn't done anything very vigorous in the water. How could it have fallen off? I would have to go out and tell the folks at the desk that I'd lost it. Paying the $41 or so didn't worry me. I wasn't sure what they would say when I told them I didn't quite remember the locker number but was sure it was one of seven. Actually, I was sure what they'd say.

I sat down on the bench and put my head in my hands. Maybe if I closed my eyes, I'd wake up in Wake Forest. Not that Iceland hadn't been wonderful, but enough was enough.

When I opened my eyes, I was still in Reykjavik, but I spotted something on the floor next to the trash can. Wonder of wonders, it was a bracelet, and it had to be mine. I scooped it up and ran to the lockers.

This was going to be easy. I'd start in the middle of what I believed to be our bank of lockers and swipe the wristband over every lock. Mine would open and voila!

The first three didn't open. I changed direction and tried the next one. Nope. The next two also didn't open. I must have chosen the wrong seven lockers. But I was sure I was in the right area. I remembered we were across from a *Do Not Wear Shoes* sign on the wall, and there it was. I tried the first locker beyond my chosen seven and swiped the bracelet over the electronic lock and—eureka!—it opened.

Relief flooded over me. I couldn't wait to get dressed and get out of there. I had no intention of ever telling anyone about this. I reached into the locker, preparing to pull out my pants and shirt, but instead found a plastic cosmetic pouch and a small Lark Tours bag, which had a tiny padlock on it. I had no idea whose locker this was, but it sure wasn't mine. The bag provided no clue because Lark Tours had given one to all of us. The only thing I knew was this locker belonged to someone in our group.

I opened the plastic pouch and peered inside. There was lip gloss, mascara, toothpaste, toothbrush, comb and a slim bottle of something called Balea. I think the instructions for use were in German, but it looked like skin lotion.

There was also a smaller opaque plastic bag, which I'm not ashamed to say I opened. It contained Advil, Tums, Claritin and a white bottle with a handwritten label that simply said KET.

I dropped it as if it were a hot coal. My heart was thumping like a basketball in my chest. Was this ketamine, the drug we were looking for? I couldn't believe it. And whose locker was this? While I debated what to do, I heard voices in the shower room. I put the medicine bag back in the pouch, stuck it in the locker and closed the door.

A voice startled me by saying, "There you are. We have to get going. Some of the others are staying here and having dinner." Olivia opened her locker and retrieved her clothes. "Christof said the bus is leaving in fifteen minutes. It's a bit of a drive back to Reykjavik, and I think he has something to do tonight." She pulled off her bathing suit and quickly donned her Capri pants and a top. "I'm skipping underwear until I can shower properly. I think I smell of sulfur."

Darn! I'd intended to stay there until the other person who lost her key tried to find it.

"Who's going back?" I asked.

"Just Angela. And Dirk, I think. All the rest are staying. I'm not quite sure how they intend to get back, but they're all having fun doing couple things."

I told Olivia I'd lost my key and couldn't get into my locker.

"You'll have to get a replacement," she said. "And you'd better hurry."

I didn't need to be told twice. In spite of violating all kinds of rules, I ran down the hall with the towel wrapped around me. Dirk was standing at the reception desk as I skidded to a stop.

He raised his eyebrows. "Something wrong?"

"I lost my key. Just have to get a replacement and I'll be on my way." The woman at the desk scowled at me but handed over another key with detailed instructions on how to use it. And I needn't have worried about forgetting my locker number. It was in their computer.

"Do you want me to come with you?" Dirk asked.

"What could you do? You can't come in the ladies locker room. But I really have something to tell you. Can we meet later this evening?" Right now wasn't a good time for a chat. I was beginning to freeze and people were staring at me.

"It would be a pleasure. We can go to a little Italian restaurant I discovered. You're sure you're okay?"

"Perfect. Toodles." I walked down the hall with as much dignity as I could muster, considering I was having a hard time keeping the towel around all the vital parts. In the dressing room, Olivia said, "Why are you looking all mushy? And you're kind of glowing. Did you just see Dirk? He's the only one who has that effect on you. Please tell me you weren't fornicating in the bushes somewhere."

"That's a ridiculous idea. I simply walked briskly down the hall. Now if you'll excuse me, I'll get dressed."

What a coincidence. My locker was right next to the one I'd opened earlier. I tried to remember who'd been beside me, but I'd been so concerned about nude bathing, I hadn't noticed.

CHAPTER TWENTY-FIVE

The Italian restaurant was cozy, full of ambience and smelled of garlic and spices. In other words, it was terrific. As I scanned the menu, I realized I wanted to order nearly everything on it. Our diet of fish and fresh vegetables was healthy and tasty enough, but I was craving tomato sauce, fried eggplant, pasta, meatballs and anything with cheese.

Dirk and I settled on calamari as an appetizer, followed by a caprese salad and spicy sausage and artichoke linguine as a main course. Armed with a satisfying glass of wine, I sat back in my seat and said, "I have a lot to tell you."

"I can't wait," he said. "Shoot."

So I told him about losing my key and opening the wrong locker and finding the bottle of ketamine.

Instead of congratulating me on a job well done, he frowned and said, "You didn't bring it with you?"

"Well, no. It never occurred to me. I wasn't really thinking of anything but getting out of there. But we don't need it, do we? I mean now we know for sure that Lydia was drugged, George and I probably were, too, and Gudrun is one of us."

Dirk twirled his pasta expertly around his fork. "I think Gudrun is laying low now. It's almost time to go home. She thinks she's almost safe. Tomorrow we have activities during the day and our farewell dinner at Perlan. After that, we go our separate ways, and she will get away with murder. Unless we can figure out a way to absolutely prove she caused Lydia's death. That's why we could have used that bottle of drugs."

"Sorry about that," I mumbled. "Maybe I'll get another chance to snatch it."

"I'm still wondering why she wants you out of the way," he said, apparently not hearing me. "You must know something and you don't realize you know it. You haven't heard anything or seen anything or found anything unusual? There *has* to be something."

"You know as much as I do. Everyone I've talked to disliked Lydia, but no one told me anything that would threaten Gudrun. I'm as confused as you are."

When we finished the last of our scrumptious dinner, Dirk ordered tiramisu and coffee.

"I think Angela must know something," I said, "But we'll never find out what it is. She's getting worse everyday."

Dirk agreed. "I know Christof is arranging to have her met by a medical team when we land at JFK. He hasn't been able to reach her contact people and is afraid to let her travel by herself."

"I don't blame him. Some of the things she says are scary. For instance, why on earth would she think you're dead?"

Dirk poured cream into his coffee. "She's in a world of her own. Maybe I remind her of someone she knew who passed away. It's impossible to figure out how her mind works."

We sat is silence for a few minutes. I desperately wished I had something—anything—that would give us a clue. I guess my mind was trying hard because I remembered the little silver ball.

"I don't know if this means anything," I said to Dirk, "but a few days ago on the bus, several bags fell on the floor and the contents spilled out. We all scrambled to retrieve our stuff. A bit later, I found a little silver ball by my foot. It had initials engraved around the center. I tucked it into my backpack, intending to show it to the ladies later, but I forgot."

Dirk looked interested. "Where is it now?"

"It's in my room. It's the only thing I can think of that's out of the ordinary, but I doubt it has anything to do with Lydia."

"What do you say we go back to your room and get it? You've aroused my curiosity."

As long as that's the only thing I'd aroused. I had no intention of being a one-night stand ever again. I didn't say that out loud though, but I did give him a look. "If we go back, we aren't going to my room. You know what I mean, in case that's what you were thinking. Besides, Olivia's there."

He laughed. "Gotcha! I'll wait in the lobby."

Once back at the hotel, true to his word, he selected a comfortable chair while I ran up to the room. Olivia was in the bathroom shampooing her hair.

"I've shampooed three times, and I still can't get that silica stuff off me. It's supposed to be beneficial, but I sure am sorry I used it." She wrapped a towel around her head and came into the bedroom. "How was dinner? Are you still smitten? Why are you dumping everything out of your backpack?"

"Good, no, and I'm looking for the little silver ball I found that day on the bus. It's not here. What do you suppose I did with it?"

"You probably put it somewhere you thought was really safe and we'll never see it again."

"Very funny," I said from inside the closet. As I plowed through all my clothes, I found the clipping I'd snatched from Lydia's suitcase. Dirk said we were looking for anything unusual so I put it in my pocket and kept looking. The silver ball was in the tote bag I'd used to carry water, snacks and energy bars on the bus.

Relieved I hadn't lost it, I yelled, "See you later!" to Olivia and ran out the door.

When I got to the lobby, Dirk was exactly where I'd left him, but now the Reillys and Alessios were back from dinner at the spa and were sitting with him. Dismayed, I shoved the ball into my pocket. We'd have to wait for a better time.

But Dirk wasn't in the mood for waiting. He stood up, took me by the hand and said, "Let's go for a walk."

I could feel raised eyebrows following us out the door. I noticed Tangerine's scowl as we exited the lobby, and it made me feel good to know she was miffed.

Dirk and I walked along the path in front of the hotel until we came to a bench under a streetlight. "Let's sit," he said, "and let me have a look at that thing."

I pulled it out and handed it to him. "I don't know what you would do with this. It's too big to hang from a necklace or bracelet, and it doesn't open, but there are initials around the middle."

Dirk weighed it in his hand. "This isn't made of silver. It's painted to look that way. It's a Chinese meditation ball. Do you hear the faint chime when I roll it in my palm? There should be two—one for each hand. People use them to relieve stress. This one was obviously personalized for someone."

I pointed to the letters. "The initials are LMB."

Dirk thought for a minute. "What about that cigarette case Angela stole from someone. It had initials on it, too. Do you remember what they were?"

"No, and there's no use asking her. I thought it was safe in my bag, but it's gone. Angela probably took it and has hidden it in a tree for a troll wife."

Dirk handed the silver ball back to me and I stuck it in my pocket. As I did so, my fingers touched the clipping. "There's also this," I said. "I found it in

Lydia's suitcase. I held it under the light and began to read: *"Douglas M. Boscoe, 31, died Friday from injuries sustained in a fall while hiking in Glacier National Park. Mr. Boscoe and his wife, Lara Boscoe..."* I stopped reading.

"Did you hear what I just said? Lara Boscoe. LB. Those are two of the initials on the ball. Do you think this article is about Lydia's brother? We know he had an accident and died. Could it be this LB is Lydia's sister-in-law?"

When Dirk didn't react, I grabbed his arm and yanked him to his feet. "Come on. Don't you want to know?"

"I do, but you're forgetting something. If this article is about Lydia's brother, then the ball could also have belonged to Lydia. LB could also be Lydia Boscoe. Her maiden name would also be Boscoe. It will depend on the middle initial."

"Sitting here isn't going to give us the answer. I'm going to find Cameron and ask him."

But finding Cameron would have to wait until tomorrow. He'd gone to bed, and there was a *Do Not Disturb* sign on his door.

CHAPTER TWENTY-SIX

Our last day in Iceland! Olivia and I kept bumping into each other as we bustled around the room collecting our belongings. I was in a hurry to pack because I was going on a whale-watching cruise with Nicole, Ginger and Tangerine. We would leave from the Old Harbour and be away for about three hours, which was perfect. Cameron was at the funeral home tying up arrangements to transport Lydia back to the States, so our questioning would have to wait until our farewell dinner tonight.

Even though I was certain one of the ladies was the evil Gudrun, the prospect of cruising with her didn't worry me. There was safety in numbers. It would have been better if Olivia had been with me, but she opted for shopping with Emma. They both wanted to buy jewelry and it seemed logical for them to go together.

As I left the hotel, I waved to Dirk, who was having coffee in the lobby. I'd come to the conclusion he was a good man, and it was too bad we lived across the country from each other.

We were lucky with the weather. The slight breeze was chilly, but the sun was warm and the water sparkled. The Old Harbour was alive with activity. People zoomed around on scooters or visited art galleries and shops in the brightly colored, renovated fishing sheds. What I loved most was the tantalizing smell of coffee. We headed to the Café Haiti, waited in line for our turn and left with what was supposed to be the best coffee in Reykjavik. We strolled slowly, sipping the delicious brew.

Our tour boat was white with a red hull. As we boarded, the captain stood on the deck and greeted us. He looked every inch the part of a seafaring sailor: white beard and white eyebrows under a black captain's hat.

We sat outside in the stern with our backs against the wall of the cabin. As we began to move, and the harbor faded away, Tangerine pointed to a hotel on the shore and said, "I stayed there back in my flight attendant days."

My ears perked right up. "You were a flight attendant?"

She nodded. "I flew for Delta for several years. Mostly overseas flights. This was one of my favorite layovers."

My, my my! I knew it! We were looking for someone who'd been to Iceland before, and here she was.

"So you must have some friends here. Maybe even know a bit of the language."

She looked at me curiously. "I suppose I do know a few people, but that's a strange question."

"Sorry. I was just wondering why you didn't mention this when we were introducing ourselves. You could have given us some tips about restaurants or shopping in Reykjavik." I needed, once again, to staple my mouth shut.

"You're beginning to annoy me, Julia. I didn't mention it because I didn't think of it."

I was dying to ask her if she was Astrid, the person the concierge had addressed in the hotel lobby, but I was afraid to keep probing.

"I don't mean to be nosy. It's just that I find this country so fascinating, I want to learn all I can about it. I'd love to be able to stay longer."

Those words nearly choked me. I couldn't wait to get home.

Nicole echoed my thoughts. "It's been fun, but I'm looking forward to leaving. I'm anxious to get Serge back to familiar surroundings."

"He's such a nice person. Is he having some kind of difficulty?" Ginger asked.

"You all probably know by now he performed surgery, which ended badly, on Mrs. Cumberland's mother," Nicole said. "Seeing Lydia on this trip was too much for him."

This was interesting. I'd never considered Serge as a suspect, but he certainly might have had a motive. But there was only one problem. He was too tall and skinny to be Gudrun.

In a sympathetic gesture, Ginger patted Nicole's knee. "He'll be fine. We're almost out of here. None of us will have to deal with Lydia Cumberland again."

For a while we sat in silence and listened to the captain tell us about the possible whale sightings and explained the difference between humpback and minke whales. I tried hard to concentrate but I had other things on my mind. I opened my mouth to speak but closed it when I saw Tangerine had tears in her eyes.

"Since we won't see each other ever again, I want to tell you something."

Oh, boy! Was this a confession? And if so, were we going to be able to subdue her if she suddenly attacked us? I looked around for help. The captain was in the wheelhouse, happily chattering away, and the only other deck crew was nowhere to be seen. I turned my attention back to Tangerine. Even though she was fit, I figured three of us should be able to take her out.

"I'm going to divorce Skip when we get back home."

What! This was not what I expected. I was stunned, but Ginger showed real concern. "I'm so sorry, Renee. You two look so happy together."

Hah! She should have witnessed what I had from the closet in their room.

Tangerine dabbed at her eyes with a tissue. "We haven't been happy for a long time. He's so dumb. He had this big dream of opening our own gym, but we have no money and haven't been able to find backers—probably because Skip is so dumb. I don't know if you've noticed but he's *always* showing off his muscles. That's all he ever thinks about. Such an exhibitionist."

Boy! Pot, kettle, black. But what did I know?

"Everything will work out for the best," Nicole said. "It seems awful now, but time heals all wounds. Is this your first marriage?"

Tangerine hesitated. "I was married before."

"Divorced?" Nicole was as nosy as I was.

Tangerine shook her head. "My husband died in an accident. It was terrible. I don't want to talk about it."

Bingo! I had my culprit. I did, however, wonder why she was giving us so many facts. We spent the rest of the trip looking for whales and yelling, "Look! There's one!" just as it disappeared under the water. When it was time to get dressed for our farewell dinner, I was sunburned and tired.

CHAPTER TWENTY-SEVEN

Perlan, or the Pearl, was a landmark building in Reykjavik. It's a glass-domed structure built over six massive hot-water storage tanks. If you could view it from the air, it would resemble a giant flower—the dome as the center and the tanks as the petals. There were three shops on the third floor, a viewing deck on the fourth and a revolving restaurant on the fifth. Christof had chosen this Icelandic icon as the place for our farewell dinner. The glass dome twinkled with hundreds of lights, and as the restaurant slowly moved, the view of Reykjavik at night was magical.

I was almost twitching as I sat down next to Dirk. "I have so much to tell you. It's definitely our friend across the table." I rolled my eyes in the direction of Tangerine. "She was married before, and her husband died in an accident. There's more, but I think we should confront her after dinner. We can get her locked up before we go home."

"Easy there, Sherlock. We're not going to accuse her of anything. If you really have proof, we'll let the police handle it. And keep your voice down. We don't need to tell everyone."

But I could hardly sit still. Here we were dressed in our best clothes and about to end our week here, and all I wanted to do was take out Tangerine. It was too bad we were dealing with a treacherous murderer in our group because Lark Tours had gone all out creating an evening to remember. We were being treated to a four-course menu, each course accompanied by an appropriate wine.

I couldn't believe my luck when Cameron sat down on the other side of me. His face was pale and he seemed unhappy, but I guessed arranging for your wife's body to be shipped home wasn't a very pleasant experience.

"I'll bet you're glad to be on your way home," I said, trying to ease into my questions.

"Not really. Lydia won't be there. And I still have to arrange a funeral and... You know what I don't understand? How did she get those drugs into her system? The police said it was a massive dose—enough to kill her, but Lydia never took anything. She was against all medications, even antibiotics."

Cameron had obviously not paid attention to all the gossip and theories. He'd heard Angela rant about hidden people and murder, but he, like most of us, hadn't given it much credence.

"I don't know, Cameron. It's a puzzle. Say, could I ask you one silly question? What was Lydia's middle name?"

He looked understandably confused. "Why do you want to know that?"

I felt color flood my face as I said, "Just curious. Names fascinate me." It sounded lame, but I couldn't think of anything else.

"Do you mean when she was young?"

"Yes. Before she was married. I'm interested in ethnic origins."

"Her name was Lydia Irene Boscoe. That doesn't tell you much about the origin of her name."

I could hardly contain myself. It told me everything I needed to know.

Christof had to be the happiest man in Iceland because he was getting rid of us tomorrow. He stood up, raised his glass and told us how much he liked the trip in spite of the "unfortunate incident." "Now please, enjoy this wonderful food and your last evening in our beautiful country. We can exchange email addresses after dinner."

The first course was smoked arctic char with a horseradish sauce, followed by a lobster bisque. "What is it with these people and fish?" Tangerine said. "When I get home I'm never eating it again."

"Do you always have to complain?" Skip speared a piece and stuck it in his mouth.

Tangerine ignored him and shot me a glance.

I nudged Dirk. "He'd better watch what he says. She might whack him, too."

Dirk sighed. "Have a sip of wine or a bite of something. Anything to keep that mouth from talking."

"Did you hear him say Lydia's middle name was Irene? How about that! The silver ball didn't belong to her."

"Eat, Julia," he said. "You need to eat and stop talking."

Since I was sure I wouldn't be eating lamb at home, I chose it for a main course, accompanied by carrots and rosemary potatoes. By the time the chocolate mousse arrived I could hardly move. Since wine had been served with every course, we were all in a mellow mood.

George stood up and tapped his glass for attention. "Just want to say this has been fun. Sorry about your wife, though, Cameron. That wasn't so good."

Good grief! The man had the sensitivity of a radish. Ginger tugged at his arm. "Sit down. You've said enough. You're going to make a fool of yourself."

"You should know how that goes, baby. You've been doing it everyday."

"You shouldn't talk to her like that," Nathan said, which surprised me.

"Do you want a piece of me, little man?" George balled his fist threateningly.

Dirk and Skip were beside him in a flash. "Hey, dude," Skip said. "Let's not make a scene in this nice place. Maybe it's time to go home. How about it, folks? Shall we go back to the hotel?"

That sounded like an excellent plan. "Go ahead," I said. "I'm going to the ladies' room and will be right down."

On a whim I went to the viewing deck on the fourth floor, figuring the lights of the city would look even more awesome outside. Surely there was also a ladies' room there. There weren't many people walking around tonight, perhaps due to a chilly wind. I located the *Dömar*—or the WC—and pushed the door open. It appeared to be deserted. But it wasn't. I heard the toilet flush in the stall next to me, and the door open. When I went to the sink to wash my hands, Ginger stood in front of the mirror applying lipstick.

"I didn't know you were in here. The rest are getting in the bus," I said.

Ginger blotted her lips on a tissue. "I'm on my way. Just wanted to have a glimpse from the deck."

I nodded in agreement. "Me, too."

"I feel sorry for Renee," she said. "Her life isn't going to be very happy for a while."

Little did she know! Soon Tangerine was going to be wearing an orange jumpsuit, or whatever color they wore in Icelandic jails.

As she turned to toss the tissue in the wastebasket, she knocked her purse off the edge of the sink, and the contents scattered all over the floor. I bent down to help her collect her things, intending to say, "Haven't we done this before?"

Instead, I held the little bottle marked KET in my hand and said nothing.

CHAPTER TWENTY-EIGHT

"Well, this is awkward," Ginger said.

"You! How can it be *you*? I was so sure it was Tangerine."

"Who?"

"Nevermind. I had it all wrong."

"I don't know what you're talking about, but I don't care." She reached up and tugged at her hair, which flew off her head and landed on the ground with the rest of her belongings. "You have no idea how much this damn thing makes me itch."

Before me stood someone I didn't know. This Ginger had short dark hair and looked completely different.

She scratched her scalp and said, "That feels better."

"I don't get it. Why did you take off your hair?"

"I just told you. My head itches. Let's talk about what we're going to do about this." She picked up her wig and put it in her bag. "I don't know why you had to be so nosy. I tried my best to get you out of the way, but you just wouldn't cooperate."

I was still shocked. "So you're Gudrun? You must be."

She wasn't listening to me. "This whole trip has been terrible. I would never have come if I'd known Lydia was Lydia Cumberland. Last I knew, her married name was Wilcox. So you see, I had no way of knowing. I read the passenger list, but it meant nothing to me."

My speech seemed to be reduced to monosyllabic words. "So why would you...?"

"Why would I not want to see her? A very simple explanation. She probably wanted some sort of silly revenge. It's a good thing I was able to buy ketamine from a doctor friend. He thought I wanted to use it to sleep, but I didn't want it for that. I wanted to use it to kill someone."

I must have looked confused because she said, "You do know who we're talking about, don't you."

"Well, I'm assuming..."

"I'm talking about Lydia." Her face was so close to mine I could feel her breath. "Lydia was on this trip for revenge. The funny thing is—I didn't recognize her. Not until our dinner the first night. She slithered up to me and said she recognized me and soon the whole world would know what I'd done."

My head was beginning to throb. "So you are..."

She gave me a patronizing look. "You are becoming tiresome. Just so you know, I am—or was—her sister-in-law. I was married to her brother. That bitch never let go of her theory that I had something to do with her brother's death." She cackled, making a sound that turned my blood to ice. "Lydia thought I pushed my husband off a cliff." She folded her arms and leaned against the sink. "I still remember the day clearly. We were hiking above the Going To The Sun Road in Glacier National Park. It was tough going, but the view was spectacular," she said with a faint smile on her face.

"Did you do it?"

The smile disappeared. "I did. I pushed him off. I told the police he tripped and fell. I had to do it, you see," she said earnestly. "He told me he had money, but he didn't, and that company he started wasn't worth a dime. He did have some life insurance, though."

I looked around frantically for a way to escape, but Ginger was between the door and me.

"I had to get rid of Lydia before she started pointing her evil finger at me. It was kind of fun to kill her the same way."

"But she had…"

"I know. She had drugs in her system. I had to give her a big dose—probably an overdose—just to make sure she stayed dead. I stuck that syringe right through her clothes. But tell me," she said conversationally, "how did you figure out it was me? Was it the meditation ball? I knew you'd found it. That's why I tried so hard to kill you. I figured you knew who I was."

I finally found my voice. "But how would I know that? And actually, I didn't figure it out. I thought it was Tangerine. I mean, I thought Tangerine was Lydia's brother's wife. But it was your sister-in-law who gave me the best clue. I found the article about your husband's death in her suitcase. Otherwise, I would never have heard of Lara Boscoe or connected the name to the initials on the ball. Even then, you might have been safe if you hadn't drugged me—and your husband. Why did you do that?"

"I just told you. You were annoying me. Especially when you didn't eat enough of that chocolate thing. As for George, I'm tired of him. He's no fun, and I don't know if you've noticed, but he's very coarse. He has no manners."

"But you seemed so meek," I said.

"Yes. I do regret that. It was easier to keep quiet because he was a bully. Sometimes I must admit, he upset me."

She was crazy. Not disoriented, spacy crazy like Angela. She was crazy dangerous. Killer crazy. And I was shaking so hard, I could hear my teeth chattering. "I have to go now," I whispered.

"Probably not. Why would I let you do that?" She pawed through her belongings on the ground until she found what she was looking for. "Ah, here it is." She picked up a gun that had slid under the sink and pointed it at me. "Get moving. I don't feel like talking anymore."

I, however, couldn't stop babbling. "And Angela? How did you get her to do all those things? And why was she afraid of Dirk?"

She scratched a spot on her scalp with the barrel of her gun. "I gave Angela small doses of ketamine—just to keep her slightly loopy. I was afraid she and her nosy friend would stumble on the truth about Lydia and me."

She pushed the gun into my back, urging me out to the viewing deck. I hoped for a brief moment that someone else was out there, but no such luck. We were alone. This was not good.

"Move across the deck, please. We don't have a lot of time. I have to get back to the bus."

"I do, too," I reminded her.

She laughed. Pointing to the railing above the water tanks, she said, "Up you go."

"You've got to be kidding."

"I'm not. You're going to climb up there and jump. Maybe you'll land safely on the tank with only broken bones, or maybe you'll break your neck, but either way you'll die because I'm going to inject you with a little something." She patted her pockets. "Doggone! I don't have my syringe. Oh well, if you're still alive after the fall, I'll shoot you."

"But won't that look like murder?" I couldn't believe I could still talk, but she chose not to hear me.

"Get climbing. I'm losing my temper."

There was nothing I could do. I hoisted myself up on the railing, looked down and was immediately dizzy.

"Now jump," she said.

"No. You're crazy." This was probably the last time in my life I'd regret not stapling my mouth shut.

"Julia, I'm not kidding around. Get going."

And with that she pushed me off, but somehow I managed to hang onto a metal rung about two feet down.

She peered over the railing. "Let go of that. You can't fall if you don't let go."

I was absolutely terrified. I screamed for help, but my voice was lost in the night and the vastness of the place.

Ginger laughed. "Go ahead and scream. No one can hear you. You remind me of Lydia."

The muscles in my shoulders burned and my fingers were nearly numb from holding on. Any minute now I would have to let go. When Ginger's face disappeared from above, pure panic swept over me. All I heard was silence. I was all alone in a strange place where I was about to plunge to my death.

Then I heard a shot. And a face appeared above the railing. "Hang on. I'm on my way to get you."

I still don't know how he did it, but in seconds he was beside me. I realized I was crying. "I can't hold on anymore. I can't feel my fingers."

"You don't have to. Let go," Dirk said. "Cameron and George are up there to pull you in."

"It isn't Tangerine," I babbled. "It's Ginger."

"We know," he said. "Stop talking. I'm going to have to touch your ass to hoist you up."

"That will be just fine," I said. I swore I heard him laugh.

CHAPTER TWENTY-NINE

We huddled in a little group outside Perlan. Every few seconds the lights from the police cars flashed across our faces, making us all a sickly blue color. I couldn't stop shaking. In spite of two shots of whatever Emma had in her flask, I was still freezing cold. And my fingers and arms ached with a pain I didn't know was possible. We tried not to look at Ginger, who sat in a police car with her head bowed.

"How did you know I was in trouble?" I asked.

"It was pure luck we found you," Dirk said. "George and Cameron were headed to the viewing deck—George was looking for Ginger, and Cameron wanted to smoke. I went with them because I was worried about you. When Ginger saw us coming toward her, she shot at us. That tipped us off that something was wrong."

"I tackled the bitch," George said. "No one shoots at me."

"When Angela saw Ginger without the wig, she screamed *Gudrun*," Dirk continued. He put his arm around me. "Guess you were wrong about the culprit."

"I guess so. I need to go to bed now because I think I'm going to fall down." With that, I closed my eyes and faded away.

I felt better the next morning. Not good, but better, and certainly eager to leave Iceland. Olivia and I shut the door to our room one final time and lugged our bags to the lobby where Dirk was waiting for us.

"How about we talk while you eat something?" he said.

"Thank you for catching me when I fainted last night," I said politely. "You seem to be rescuing me a lot lately."

"No problem. I enjoy it. I must say, I don't think I've ever met anyone who gets herself into more trouble."

Was that supposed to be a compliment? I didn't know, so I filled my plate with eggs and waffles and sat down at a table. "Where's Ginger?" I asked when we were all seated.

Dirk buttered a piece of toast. "She's in jail. Turns out she was actually born in Iceland, and her real name is Lara Astrid Magnusdottir. She was working for an international tourist company when she met Douglas Boscoe. Ginger's brother owns the house you visited in town. He helped her get Angela in all those improbable situations. Remember the tree incident? He provided the ladder. Oh, and by the way, she's going to be extradited to the US to stand trial for the murder of Lydia's brother."

I tasted the eggs and found I was hungry. "How did Angela meet Gudrun?" I asked between bites.

"Angela was in Glacier National Park on a tour when Ginger's husband died. She didn't know the couple well but had seen them in the lodge. Apparently, Mr. Boscoe physically resembled me, which is why Angela kept insisting I was dead. She must have somehow seen Ginger without the wig and recognized her. Ginger managed to convince her she was someone named Gudrun. It can't have been difficult to mess with Angela's mind."

"What was the deal with the wig?" Olivia asked. "And the name, Ginger? That was obviously an alias."

Dirk shrugged. "George said she thought it was a kick for them to have the same hair color. Who knows? As far as the name goes, aren't redheads sometimes called Ginger? I'm sure she thought it was very clever."

This was amazing. I poured myself more coffee and picked up a sweet roll at the breakfast buffet. "Here's the big question," I said when I sat back down. "Lydia made the reservations for this trip at the last minute. Obviously, she had intended some kind of unpleasantness for Ginger. But how did Lydia know her-sister-in-law would be on the trip?"

"Lydia had been keeping track of Ginger ever since her brother died. I think her desire for revenge had been festering for years. A friend of Lydia's, who knew the whole story, works for Lark Tours. She happened to see Ginger's name on the reservation list and sent it to Lydia. It sounds improbable, but that's how the Cumberlands happened to be on the tour. You remember Cameron saying this wasn't something Lydia would usually do."

I went back to the buffet table and helped myself to some smoked salmon and two slices of wonderful bread. The Nordic Hilton put out quite a spread. Back at the table, I put horseradish sauce and onions on the fish. "So what is Emma's problem? She hasn't seemed normal either."

"Oh, she's an alcoholic," Olivia said. "I've known that for quite a while. She has booze stuffed all over her luggage, but she's harmless. She was just afraid we'd discover what most of us already knew so she wrote that note to try to scare us off."

"And the rest of the folks?" I asked.

"The Alessios are taking different flights home," Dirk said. "His wife forgot to tell him she was planning to file for divorce. He was not happy. The others are okay. Cameron has already left for the airport with his wife's body."

Well, then. There was nothing left to do but leave. As we headed to the door, Dirk said, "Can I talk to you for a minute, Julia?"

Olivia gave him a wave and headed to the bus. "I just want you to know this has been a wonderful week for me." When I raised my eyebrows, he said, "Maybe we could have done without parts of it, but I'm so happy I came on this trip." He paused. "Because I met you."

Was I still breathing? I couldn't speak, and this time my mouth wasn't stapled shut.

"I also want you to know that evening in my room was wonderful. I never mentioned it because I was afraid you'd think I was being sappy if I told you how much I liked you. I haven't done anything like that since my bachelor days before I was married."

"Me neither," I managed to croak. "Actually, not ever."

At that moment, Christof hurried across the lobby and urged us to get on the bus. "Time to go, folks."

Dirk pulled me into a hug. "This isn't the end. We'll stay in touch. California isn't that far away."

I smiled. It was, but I wasn't going to argue with him.

"Call me if you need someone to hoist you out of trouble."

"You bet," I said as I climbed on the bus. "I'm very selective about who touches my ass."

THREE MONTHS LATER

At this time of day, the sun was low enough in the sky to cast a lovely orange glow over the sand and palmetto trees in Sea Pines. Out in the ocean, dolphins cavorted, and a pelican swooped down to catch fish.

I sat on the deck of the gorgeous rental home and thought about the last few months. Never in a million years did I ever dream that taking that trip to Iceland would change my life. I was happier now than I'd been since, well, since before Tony died.

When my cell phone rang I was so content I debated not answering, but Olivia was calling, and there might be a problem at Little Bites.

"Are you enjoying your long weekend?" she asked.

"I am. Everything okay back there?"

"Yes, but we sold out of all those fancy cupcakes you made. Even the ones in the freezer."

I closed my eyes. I didn't want to think about cupcakes or work at the moment. "There's a three-layer chocolate marshmallow cake in a box in the back behind the ice cream. Cut it into small pieces and serve that. I'll be back on Tuesday," I told her.

"Got it. Anything else new?"

The front door banged shut and I heard footsteps on the tile floor. "Nope. I'll see you soon. I have to go now. Dinner just arrived."

Dirk walked toward me carrying a container of steamed shrimp and a bottle of wine.

THE END

ABOUT THE AUTHOR

 Linda S. Clayton has been writing ever since she could hold a pencil. She wrote a poem for *Jack and Jill*, class songs, a college class play—The History of Hair, a book about her sister's many glorious hair colors and styles, and many other mostly forgettable things.

During the thirty years she and her husband lived overseas, Linda had a successful career as a portrait painter, but she never stopped writing. She wrote a humor column for an English publication in Bonn, Germany, and wrote countless attempts at novels that were shoved in the back of a drawer. Her adventures and misadventures in foreign countries are providing a steady supply of material for her new Julia Greene Travel Mysteries.

Linda loves to grow vegetables—particularly tomatoes, travel, and play with her two dogs.

www.ingramcontent.com/pod-product-compliance
Lightning Source LLC
Chambersburg PA
CBHW050422260626
47156CB00003B/1124